DARKNESS
SHALL FALL

ZONDERVAN

Darkness Shall Fall
Copyright © 2011 by Alister McGrath
Illustrations © 2011 by Wojciech Nowakowski, Bartosz Nowakowski, and Marta
Nowakowska

This title is also available as a Zondervan ebook.
Visit www.zondervan.com/ebooks

Requests for information should be addressed to:

Zonderkidz, 5300 *Patterson Ave SE, Grand Rapids, Michigan* 49530

This edition: ISBN 978-0-310-72194-9 (softcover)

ISBN 978-0-310-71814-7 (hardcover)

Published in association with the literary agency of Alive Communications, Inc.,
7680 Goddard Street, Suite 200, Colorado Springs, CO 80920.
www.alivecommunications.com.

Art direction: Kristine Nelson
Cover design: Sarah Molegraaf
Interior design and composition: Luke Daab, Carlos Eluterio Estrada,
Greg Johnson/Textbook Perfect

Printed in the United States of America

12 13 14 15 16 17 /DCI/ 22 21 20 19 18 17 16 15 14 13 12 11 10 9 8 7 6 5 4 3 2 1

THE AEDYN CHRONICLES

BOOK THREE

DARKNESS SHALL FALL

Alister McGrath

ZONDERVAN.com/
AUTHORTRACKER
follow your favorite authors

CHAPTER

1

"How far will it spread?" Gregory asked.

Peter Grant didn't take his eyes off the monstrous black cloud billowing from the volcano over the island of Khemia. "I don't know," Peter said. "Maybe it will cover the whole sky."

The two friends stood on a slight rise in the forest, gazing beyond the trees, across the island, at the volcano. An orange glow marked its mouth, where lava still spewed in a slow, torrential flow. Above the volcano the haze of spreading darkness was evident even in the moonlight, like an ink stain spreading across the night sky, blotting out the stars.

"Scientists believe that a cloud like this wiped out the dinosaurs," Peter said, his eyes mesmerized by the ever-growing dark haze of ash rising above the volcano. "Only it wasn't from a volcano, but a massive asteroid that struck the ocean just off the Yucatan Peninsula sixty-five million years ago. Gregory, are you even listening to me?"

But Gregory's gaze had drifted toward the ground where he was busy foraging. "I'm trying not to," he said.

Peter stepped down off the ridge and joined Gregory's search of the forest floor. "Well, you should listen. Science is what separates us from the lower mammals."

"Hopefully I *am* the only one listening to you," Gregory hissed. "Keep your voice down, already."

"Right," Peter whispered, scanning the moonlit forest as if Gul'nog might swarm them any moment. "I forgot." Before his transport from London to the mysterious world of Aedyn and the island of Khemia, he'd never had to worry about such things.

Gregory pointed. "There!"

Peter ducked. "You see one?"

In the darkness, the outline of Gregory's arm was barely visible. "At least one," he said. He strode forward and knelt beside something on the turf.

Peter's heart thumped in his chest. *A Gul'nog? Here?* Before Peter had time to react, Gregory pulled his small knife—and sliced at the dirt. Peter almost laughed in relief. It wasn't one of the horrible, eight-feet-tall creatures ready to tear their limbs off. Gregory had found a fungus. Fungi.

Mushrooms, to be exact.

"Bring me your bag." Gregory cut the mushrooms with his small knife and dropped them into Peter's canvas sack. He wiped the blade and slid it back into the leather scabbard on his belt.

"How many, Gregory?" Peter was still spooked, so he kept his voice soft in his companion's ear.

"Twelve."

Peter's shoulders dropped a little. "All right," he said. "Let's find the others. Maybe they've had better luck."

They rose and went back the way they had come. They knew these woods—knew how to pass through without being heard. They knew how to move with the shadows, slipping in between the branches of the trees like wraiths. They knew where it was safe to step and where a misplaced foot might suck a man into a hidden bog. They had wandered these woods every night for two months.

The shadow—the volcano cloud—spread every day, nearly reaching the horizon, growing thicker and blacker. Even in the daylight it blocked out the sun, leaving the landscape an ashen, dirty gray. Not that they'd seen it in daylight lately. It had been weeks since they had been outside during the day.

A twig snapped, and Gregory put out an arm, stopping Peter in his tracks. They waited, trying not to breathe. Peter prayed they were downwind of anything that could sniff them out.

Another snap, and another. Something was out there. And it was getting closer.

Only two steps away from Peter stood a great tree, its trunk so thick that both he and Gregory could not have reached around it. Peter crouched low and curled himself tightly into a ball, nestling himself between two of the massive tree roots. Though Gregory made no sound, Peter saw that he had done the same.

They waited there, Peter hardly breathing, willing his heart to stop pounding. But the footsteps grew closer.

Whoever or whatever it was moved slowly—too slowly just to be passing by. It must have been searching for something. Or someone.

Peter risked a peek. There, not more than twenty feet from the place where they crouched, a creature of Shadow lifted its head and drank in the stale air of the forest. It listened, sniffing, breathing in the scent of man. With dread sinking deep into his stomach, Peter realized the truth: it was a Gul'nog, and it knew they were there.

In the dark months since Peter had first come to Khemia, he had grown to fear these monsters more and more. They thrived on the stale, acrid air of the place,

growing stronger as the days pressed on. The Gul'nog
were monsters out of some nightmare—their skin
marked by welts and scars, their massive limbs the size
of small trees. Peter sometimes thought they looked like
gnarled old trees themselves.

    The Gul'nog were the reason for these midnight
raids. Peter and a small band of men went out each evening, foraging for food and unspoiled water for those
who had lived through the volcano blast. Not one of the
refugees ever forgot that the only reason they were still

alive was that the Gul'nog had not yet discovered their
hiding place.

But the monsters knew they were still on the
island—knew that some of them had survived the
eruption—and so they searched.

Peter willed himself to become smaller as he
shrank back into the tree's roots. The bark cut into his
skin. It was always this way when the Gul'nog were
near—always this paralyzing fear.

Peter watched in horror as the monster's head
turned toward them. The Gul'nog's lips curled up in a
snarl as it started forward. Heaven help him: the monster had picked up their scent. It was coming for them.

Should they wait here to die or try to run? Peter
had escaped from a Gul'nog once before by staying
hidden in the trees and then ducking into a cave, but
the only cave nearby—the only cave he could get to in
time—was the cave where Peter's sister, Julia, his stepsister, Louisa, and the remnant of the people of Aedyn
were hiding. Peter squeezed his eyes shut tight and
prayed that death would be quick.

Then the Gul'nog was upon them.

It reached Gregory first. Its fist came out and
gripped Gregory's arm in a death vice, squeezing
until he cried out in agony. Peter could hear the bones
crunching.

A strange thought leapt into his mind: *Leave Gregory! The thing will start eating him, and you'll have time to get away.*

He pulled his feet beneath him and actually sprang up to flee.

The Gul'nog whipped around to face him, surprised. But it quickly recovered and snarled at Peter.

His moment to escape was gone. Whether it was an act of heroism or because he had no other choice, Peter leapt forward and lashed out at the monster. It dropped Gregory and squared off against Peter.

This was it. He was going to be ripped to pieces and eaten by a—his thoughts cut off suddenly as there came a low, rumbling bellow. Peter felt the sound as much as he heard it. It reverberated inside his skin, shaking him to his bones, and he dropped to the ground. It was an alien noise, foreign to his ears, and he shuddered at its force.

At the sound, the Gul'nog lifted its head, and answering some call that only he seemed to understand, turned from Peter and ran through the trees the way he had come.

Peter's pulse raced, and more than a few moments passed before he could breathe again.

"Peter?" Gregory's whisper was so quiet it might have been a leaf quivering on the wind.

"It's all right now," Peter said, dizzy with shame at nearly leaving his friend to save himself. Was he becoming just as bad as the evil creatures who hunted them? "Thought we were done for."

"And *I* thought—ow!" Gregory grabbed at his shoulder and dropped to his knees.

"Your arm!" Peter stood, brushed the broken bark and twigs off his clothing, and reached out a hand.

"Broken, I think," said Gregory, biting his tongue between his teeth. "I'll be all right. We have to get back—find the others."

Peter grasped Gregory's good arm and helped him to his feet.

"Don't forget the mushrooms."

"Right." Peter grabbed the bag from the ground.

"What made it leave?" Gregory asked through gritted teeth.

"Some sort of horn, I think." Gregory stumbled and Peter grabbed his bad arm, causing Gregory to cry out in pain.

They made their way through the dense forest for another ten minutes. Peter knew Gregory would be going into shock soon—if he hadn't already—though he continued forward. At length, they emerged into a small clearing, on the edges of which waited a group of bedraggled men. The other foragers. They brightened when they saw Peter and Gregory coming in from the trees.

"We heard somethin.   st," Orrin said.
"We thought—"

"We had some trouble," Pete.   nodding to
Gregory. He scanned the group. "Are all re.urned?"

Orrin nodded. "Not much but leaves, nuts, and
mushrooms."

Peter sighed. It had not, he thought ruefully, been
a good night for foraging. But no matter about that—
the Gul'nog knew their area now. A full search party
would probably be arriving soon. They would have to
move again. And Gregory needed care. They had to get
back to the others.

The ten men walked single file, making their way
through the shadows and back to the cave. Peter could
hear Gregory panting and hissing, evidently in great
pain. But Gregory kept the agony to himself. If only they
could all be so strong.

The last move had almost been too much for
some of the younger children, and he was loath to
attempt another so soon. Peter pushed the thought from
his mind as he approached the cave entrance hidden
deep in the crags of the cliff. Again he marveled that the
cliff face in front of him concealed its entrance. It looked
like bare rock to him, with only the occasional spray
of vines here and there. If he hadn't already known its
location, he never would have found it in the darkness.
Peter squeezed sideways through the narrow opening,

shimmying between the tight walls of rock that closed him in on either side. In a strange way, it was a good thing they were running out of food. If they'd been feasting every day, they wouldn't be able to get in or out of their hideout. It was some small comfort that no Gul'nog would be able to squeeze through the opening. Though the monsters would probably just toss a few lit torches inside and smoke them out. He tried not to think about that.

Perhaps you've explored a large cave before. If so, you know the feeling of weight that crushes in, around you and over you, especially if you have to squeeze through a tight spot. You get the feeling that if you become stuck, there will be no rescue. It's not like someone can just take the cave walls away to pull you free. That's how Peter felt as he scraped along the passage.

There was a dampness in the tunnel that turned his lungs into a sponge, soaking in the stale, wet air. He held his breath, trying not to think of the word "coffin" as he pushed himself through the passage's twists and turns. Finally, the tunnel opened into a large, open room lit by a fire. Not quite cheery, but warm nonetheless.

The smoke worried them at first. Would it suffocate them? Or waft skyward and signal their location to the Gul'nog? But evidently narrow flues and crannies made the smoke dissipate and carried it far enough away so that it had not revealed their location. *Yet.*

Peter stepped into the central room and found himself confronted by a young woman, her blonde hair falling around her shoulders and her face flushed red from the great fire in the center of the cavern.

"Well?" she demanded, hands planted firmly on her hips. "What did you find?"

CHAPTER

2

Peter cleared his throat as he regarded his sister. After the long silence of the woods, he never felt comfortable speaking aloud. "We didn't find much," he said simply. "We ... we weren't able to stay as long as we'd hoped."

"Why not?" Julia asked. "What happened?"

Peter stepped aside as Gregory and some of the others pushed through into the chamber.

"Gregory," Julia said, "what did you bring?"

Gregory shrugged, then grimaced and held his shoulder.

"What happened to you?" Julia asked.

"I'll be fine," Gregory said, waving her away.

Peter collected the bags from Gregory and the other foragers and laid them on the cook table. "There isn't much left."

Julia's hand went to her mouth. "It's not enough! Not nearly enough." She stared at Peter accusingly. "There must be more food somewhere. There must be some plants we can eat, or rabbits or something. You're just not looking hard enough. Tomorrow night ... tomorrow you'll have to keep looking."

She was using her snotty-little-sister voice. Had the situation been different, Peter might well have yelled back at her. But he just shook his head. "We can't look for food tomorrow night. Tomorrow night we'll probably be moving to a new hideout."

Julia looked alarmed. "What? But we just got moved in. Why would we have to—oh!"

"We were chased tonight," Peter said. He eased Gregory onto a stool. "A Gul'nog was out in the woods. It spotted us. Grabbed Gregory." He thought again of his temptation to flee. Had the creature not seen him, would he have sacrificed Gregory to save himself? "Anyway, it was close to the cave—close enough for him to find it if he brings friends and comes looking again. We'll have to be on the lookout."

Julia went to Gregory and touched his shoulder gently. "But how on earth did you escape?"

Peter and Gregory exchanged glances. The other foragers had moved off to their sleeping areas, but they were still close enough to hear.

"We ... um ...," Gregory said.

"Something scared it away," Peter said. "Or called it away. Some signal horn, best I can figure. It went one way, and we went the other. But not before it had just about pulled Gregory's arm off."

Julia nodded resolutely. "All right then, we'll organize a watch. We can take turns waiting at the mouth of the cave. The guard will sound the alert if ... if anything should come. Now Gregory, let's get you taken care of."

By the light of the fire, Peter could see that Julia's cheeks were drawn. She was beyond tired, he thought, exhausted from the long weeks of strain and uncertainty. They all were.

Peter left his sister and withdrew to an outcropping of rock on the other side of the fire. It was colder here, and the air was wetter, but at least it was private. Here, he could have space to think.

It had been two months—eight long, unending weeks—since the volcano had erupted, spewing toxic fumes into the air and killing so many of the good people of Aedyn. Many of the bad people too, including Captain Ceres and his henchmen. Peter felt it was up to him and Julia to get the remaining survivors off this

cursed island of Khemia and return them to the land
they knew first, the land the Lord of Hosts had created
for these men, women, and children. Aedyn.

In the days before the eruption, Peter thought
he had found a way. An ancient prophecy told of a talisman — a talisman that would bring back the Lord of
Hosts and defeat the darkness once and for all, *if* the two
halves of the talisman were united. They had retrieved
part of the talisman from Captain Ceres, and then Julia
had discovered the other half of the talisman back in her
bedroom at her grandmother's house in London. Her
grandmother had found it in her garden and had given
Julia the pendant. Peter pressed his fists hard into his
eyes at the memory and fought back the tears of frustra-
tion that stung their surface.

It should have worked — it was *supposed* to have
worked. But when he and Julia had pressed the two
halves of the talisman together, there was no music, no
bells, no blinding light. Nothing. And the Shadow had
eclipsed the sky just the same, as if there had been no
prophecy or talisman. As if the Lord of Hosts had abandoned them after all.

Peter could feel people gazing at him. The foragers and the rest of the survivors stood scattered about
the cavern now, talking quietly in small groups of five or
six. Their shadows danced on the walls of the cave. The
people of Aedyn had believed in him. He'd promised

them he'd had a plan—and they had trusted him. But now they knew he was just as lost and confused as the rest of them.

Movement caught his attention—a slim girl with gray eyes and golden hair. She moved gracefully among the people, kneeling beside one, laying a cool hand on the fevered forehead of another.

Louisa.

She seemed to be the only one unaffected by the air of this place. Since the eruption of the volcano she had grown only gentler and more joyful. *Joy*, Peter scoffed. What had any of them to be joyful about? But he couldn't deny the transformation that had taken place in his stepsister.

When the three of them first came to Aedyn together, tumbling into an icy stream and through the portal, Louisa had done little but weep and faint and carry on. She had been, frankly, quite impossible—nearly as beastly as when they'd been back home. But since the eruption she had not wept once. And the people seemed to trust her. She moved among them, calming their fears with words of comfort. She seemed able to reassure them in a way that Peter and Julia, who had fancied themselves Deliverers, could not. But how *could* they be Deliverers? Were they not mere teenagers, barely able to care for themselves back in London, let alone a cavern full of suffering survivors?

Peter stretched out his hand and felt for a ledge
in the rock. It was small—no bigger than the width of
his fist—but over the centuries the water had dripped
off its edge and hollowed out a tiny space underneath.
Peter reached into the puddle and felt for the cool metal
under his fingertips. Grasping the talisman, he brought
it up close to his face where he could study it.

The light was too dim to see the details, but Peter
already knew it by heart. He turned it over and over in
his hand. Since the day of the eruption, it had begun to
glow with a strange blue light. You couldn't see the glow

unless it was utterly dark, but it was there. The talisman was in the shape of a hexagon with two long sides, and inside the outer piece was a star with six points. When the two shapes were brought together, snapped together like two pieces of a puzzle, they were supposed to summon the Lord of Hosts—at least according to the prophecy. Only it hadn't worked.

Maybe there was more to the prophecy, Peter thought. Maybe there were magic words that ought to be spoken, or maybe one ought to turn around three times and spit before uniting the pieces. Or maybe, thought Peter, a little despairingly, the prophecy had been nothing but a fairy tale all along.

Peter tucked the talisman back into its hiding place and tried to go to sleep.

It was morning when he woke. The fire had died down to a mess of smoldering ashes, and someone—Gregory—was feeding it kindling and branches to bring it back to life. There was no shortage of wood on the island, Peter thought. At least that was something they could be thankful for.

He rubbed the morning from his eyes and swung his legs off the ledge and onto the rocky floor beneath. People lay sleeping on the ground, curled up under threadbare blankets and cloaks. Eighty-seven of them in all—men, women, and children who had survived the blast, found each other amidst the confusion, and made it to safety together. Eighty-seven. Plus three young strangers from another world.

Julia sat cross-legged in the far corner of the room, close to the entrance to the tunnel. Peter made his way over to her and plunked himself down beside her. She had her knees tucked under her chin and her arms wrapped around her legs. She seemed very deep in thought.

"You on watch?" he asked.

Julia shook her head. "James is out front. He's staying just inside the cave—close enough to sound the alarm if the Gul'nog come." She shivered, and her big eyes looked up at her brother. "I don't know what we'd do if they found us. There's nowhere to run—nowhere to retreat."

"I know," Peter said. "I've never liked that this place has no back door. Maybe we can find one that does."

"But where could we move, Peter? We'd have to scout out a new cave, and you remember how awful it was to move the children last time. Trying to keep them quiet."

Peter nodded.

"We have to get them all back to Aedyn," Julia said. "*That's* what they need, not another smelly, old cave. Going home is what they expect. It's what the Lord of Hosts brought us here to do, right?"

They'd had this conversation before—gone over the possibilities a hundred times. It all came down to boats. The eruption had destroyed all the Gul'nog ships, and if there was a way to build a seafaring vessel large enough to carry ninety people—under cover of darkness and without a Gul'nog noticing—without a lick of knowledge about shipbuilding or navigation between them, he didn't know what it was.

There came the sounds of stirring behind them. The people were beginning to awaken, their bellies rumbling and their throats parched. They wouldn't complain—except for the children—but Peter and Julia would see the disappointment in their eyes. Peter put his arm around his sister, and she laid her head on his shoulder. Not for the first time, he wished they had never been taken from London into this strange, new land.

They sat for a moment like that, and then they both lifted their heads at the sound of footsteps coming from the tunnel. Peter leapt to his feet, prepared for any sort of villain to appear. He wished he had Gregory's knife, at least. They really ought to make more weapons.

It turned out to be only James. But his face had gone absolutely white.

"What is it?" Peter asked. "Did you see something?"

James simply stepped aside mutely, and it was then that Peter realized he was not alone.

Behind him, just coming out of the tunnel, was another man, tall and muscular, with waves of golden hair that fell around his shoulders.

Peter blinked at him. "Who are you?"

"I've come from the Lord of Hosts," the stranger said. "I thought you were expecting me."

CHAPTER

3

The stranger stood there for a long moment, a bemused smile playing across his face. "My name is Peras. You were waiting for help ... yes?"

Peter clenched his fists, ready for anything. "Where did you come from?" he asked, his eyes narrowing. "If you've really been sent by the Lord of Hosts—"

"Why did I take so long?" The stranger kept his eyes on Peter, ignoring the curious crowd that was gathering behind him. "Khemia isn't an easy place to get to. I've been journeying to get here ever since you and your sister put the two parts of the talisman back together."

He knew about the talisman. So it *had* worked after all. With relief flooding through him, Peter unclenched his hands and reached out to grasp Peras's hand in his own. "Welcome! You are welcome to this place." Peter turned to address the group.

But Peras held up his hands and spoke. "I bring you greetings from the Lord of Hosts," he cried out in a strong voice—a voice that was too loud for the small cave. His words echoed off the close walls of the chamber and reverberated around the stone chamber. "I have come to set you free from the Shadow and to bring you back to the land you knew first—Aedyn."

He continued to speak, but no one could hear his words so loud were the cheers. The people crowded around Peras, peppering him with questions and shaking his hand. If there had been room, they might've hoisted him to their shoulders and paraded him around the chamber—and Peter would've led them. He'd struck out as a Deliverer, so it was good to have one for himself.

"What's this?"

A displeased voice cut through the hubbub. Peter looked up and saw Louisa just entering from a side chamber. Her eyes were afire with some emotion. He didn't know what it was, but it didn't look like joy. If he didn't know better, he'd say it was fear.

"Louisa!" He rushed over to her. "This is Peras. He's a servant of the Lord of Hosts. He came when we activated the talisman. He's come to take the people home!"

The crowd rejoiced again at his words. They might've gone on with their celebration had Louisa not thrown a damper on it again.

"So he just appears at our cave saying he's from the Lord of Hosts, and you believe him?"

Peter felt the happiness draining out of him. "Well ..."

"All of you," Louisa said to the people of Aedyn. "How do you know you can trust this ... person?"

"Louisa," Peter said, turning away from the group, "please, you're making a scene. How else could he have found us if he weren't from the Lord of Hosts?"

"How could he find us?" she said very loudly. "Word has reached my ears that you and Gregory were discovered by the enemy only yesterday. Our retreat is no longer hidden, Peter. It wouldn't be just the Lord of Hosts who could find us now."

Peter looked at Louisa. He'd never known her to be like this. Petulant and awful before, but mainly kind and peaceful since coming here. What had gotten into her now? He looked at her drawn, white face. Her eyes narrowed even further as she looked at the newcomer in their cave. What if—

Peras held up his hands to silence the crowd that stood gathered around him. A hush fell over them, and a smile spread over his lips. "Dear girl, you have nothing to fear. I come from the throne of the Lord of Hosts in

this, your hour of need." He turned his benevolent gaze to the others. "As you know, the ships were destroyed. And the Gul'nog are never far. Indeed, they are close to discovering your hiding place once again, as you have said." His eyes were on Louisa. "I have come to help you build new ships. I will take you back to Aedyn, where the Shadow will never find you again."

Of course, Peter thought. New ships. At last, someone who could teach them how to build and sail.

"Why should we believe you?" Louisa asked, spoiling everything again. "We do not know you. Nor do we know that the Shadow has not spread over Aedyn as well. We can see it moving across the horizon. Who are you to say that Aedyn is any safer than this island—or this cave?"

"I am Peras," the stranger all but shouted. "I speak with the authority of the Lord of Hosts. You will obey— excuse me. You will *believe* me because I am His servant."

There was a long moment in which a silence pressed against the people. Peter wondered whether or not it would be wise to speak.

Louisa's gaze never weakened. She turned that glare from Peras to Peter. "Mark my words, brother, Peras will betray us all."

"Hush, Louisa!" Peter said. "You don't know what you're saying." He looked back at their savior, Peras, who finally took his eyes from Louisa.

"Come, Peter. Bring your bravest men. We must plan your escape."

Peras chose ten of the men—Peter, Gregory, Orrin, and the rest of the midnight foragers. Together they went to the fire and talked long into the night.

Julia couldn't sleep. She turned first one way, then the other, willing herself to fall quickly and dreamlessly to sleep. But the rock floor seemed harder than usual, her threadbare blanket couldn't keep her warm, and the constant *drip-drip-drip* of the stalactites pounded in her head.

She thought longingly of her bed at home—thought of sinking deep into that pile of blankets and pillows. She grunted and rolled over on her side, trying to adjust to a new position. Some things, she decided, you just couldn't appreciate until they were gone.

No one seemed to be sleeping much. Peras and his band of men—Peter among them—were huddled around the fire. The flames lent their faces an otherworldly glow and threw their shadows up against the walls of the cave. Their voices were hushed, punctuated with the occasional burst of harsh laughter. Julia did not like the sound of that laughter. Nor was she accustomed to being left out of things. Gaius hadn't left her out.

Gaius. Julia made a sound that might have been a snort as she rolled over once again. Gaius had been the one to call them all to Aedyn in the first place. He had said they were the Deliverers and had shown them how to defeat the three dark lords who had held Aedyn captive in their mighty grip. And then, not long after the people had been freed, Gaius had called Peter, Julia, and now Louisa, through the portal and into the lives of the people of Aedyn once again. Only this time the task had not been so easy.

The people had been taken captive and brought to the island of Khemia by Captain Ceres and the

Gul'nog. They'd been forced to dig at the base of a volcano, searching for something they'd never been told
about. Their masters had been cruel, and the people had
wilted under their whips.

Gaius had come to help only at the end, giving
Julia a way to return home and retrieve the missing
piece of the talisman. Sometimes she wondered if she'd
seen him at all. He certainly hadn't bothered to show
his face since.

Gaius, where are you? Won't you come now?

Julia tilted her head and saw that someone else
was still awake. Louisa was back in the far corner of the
cave, speaking softly and leaning over someone in the
darkness. It must be Gregory, still in pain from his en-
counter with the Gul'nog.

Julia watched her stepsister for a moment. Louisa
moved slowly and deliberately, placing her hand on the
patient's forehead for a moment, adjusting his bandages,
bending to speak a soft word in his ear.

Perhaps Louisa felt Julia watching her, for she
lifted her head and smiled in her direction. The smile
was weak—almost piteous. It was so odd how she'd op-
posed Peras like that.

Julia rose to her feet, pulling what remained of
the blanket tightly around her shoulders. She stepped
over the slumbering bodies of the people of Aedyn and
picked her way over to Louisa.

The patient was indeed Gregory. He was sleeping fitfully, drifting in and out of consciousness. He seemed to calm only at Louisa's touch. But Louisa looked as if she could use a healer herself. Her face was drawn and pale, and the violet circles under her eyes testified that she had not slept in days. Still, there was an air of serenity about her that Julia couldn't understand.

Here was Louisa, her horrid stepsister, who in the best of circumstances was one of the nastiest human beings Julia had ever had the pleasure to meet. But plunk her in a rotten dung hole of a place, and she was utterly transformed. She had become ... well, it wasn't for nothing that the people had begun to call her the Healer.

"I would have thought you'd be over by the fire," Louisa said, raising her head as Julia approached. "Over with Peras and Peter and the others. Plotting our 'rescue.'"

"Peras didn't pick me," Julia said, trying—but not quite managing—to force out a hollow laugh. "I suppose I'm not the Chosen One anymore."

Louisa's expression didn't change as she looked toward the fire and the men sitting around it. "No," she said, a strange note in her voice. "Peras has chosen only the strongest for his little army."

"But it's not an army," Julia said. "You don't understand. He's here to help us escape—not fight. He's going to help us build boats and show us the way back to Aedyn."

Louisa was curiously silent. Her lips pursed tightly together and she shook her head once. "Whether he uses our own men or … others … he's definitely going to raise up an army."

"Against the Gul'nog?"

"No, silly. Against me."

CHAPTER

4

"Against *you*?" Julia finally said. "But ... but you're nobody. No offense. I mean, you're not from here, and you weren't called like we were. You only came here by accident in the first place, because you followed us to get us in trouble."

Louisa smiled that pitying smile again and returned to her patient.

Julia sighed and left Louisa there, picking her way back through the slumbering bodies to her spot not far from the fire. The men were all still there, squatting close by the flames, but only Peras seemed to be talking now. Whispering, almost. Julia strained to hear but couldn't catch more than the occasional word.

She was too exhausted to stay awake any longer. She'd have to ask Peter to explain it all in the morning. Her stomach grumbled, but Julia pressed the hunger from her mind, rolled over, and fell into a fitful sleep.

Peter watched Peras closely, all of his hopes hanging on every word Peras spoke. Finally—finally, here was the deliverance they'd all been praying for. And Peter, who had fancied himself the Chosen One, had never been so delighted to be relieved of responsibility.

"The Shadow has not spread far yet," Peras said in those gentle, soothing tones. "Not as far as Aedyn's borders. But we haven't much time. Where the Shadow goes, so go the Gul'nog. It has already overtaken the islands of Melita and Tunbridge."

"What will happen when it reaches Aedyn?" Peter asked. "Will you help us fight?"

"The Shadow will not spread so far," Peras answered, waving his hand as if to wipe away the question.

"But if—"

"Trust me, Peter," Peras said.

So Peter did.

"We'll build rafts during the night and sleep during the day," Peras said to the men. "We'll need to gather materials outside the cave without being detected, but

it seems you are already skilled at avoiding the Gul'nog."
He winked at Peter. "Once the rafts are ready," Peras said,
"you nine—and myself—will each captain one. I'll lead
you all back to Aedyn. I know the way."

Peter heaved a sigh of relief. Thank goodness for
that talisman. It had brought Peras to them, and without
Peras they would have been lost indeed. "I'll lead the
foraging raids," Peter said. "If you'll just tell me what to
look for, we'll find it—so long as it isn't mushrooms."

"No mushrooms," Peras said with a smile. "I'll
handle the food. The Lord of Hosts provides for His
children."

No more mushrooms! Just wait until Julia hears
this. Peter sat back with a grin. This Peras was turning
out to be a fine fellow—a very fine fellow indeed.

"Sticks, sticks, sticks," Peter said, looking around the forest floor. "Sticks and vines, sticks and vines."

"That one's not big enough," Orrin said.

Peter turned it over in his hand, sizing it up with
his not-yet-practiced eye, and threw it off into the brush.

"*Shh!*" Orrin hissed. "You never know where
they'll be."

"Not here," Peter said. "They've stopped patrolling
this area. Haven't seen a Gul'nog since Peras came."

"You don't know they've stopped. They could be planning anything. I just—I don't think a little caution would be out of place."

Peter nodded. He'd be quiet and keep Orrin happy, but he knew he was safe now. They were all safe. He felt it deep in his bones: the danger had passed now that Peras had come.

Peter stumbled over another stick and bent to pick it up. It was larger this time. Large enough to use, according to Orrin's affirming nod. Peter added it to their pile—gently this time.

They had quite the pile built up. It was a better haul than last night's. They were looking for sticks and logs to build the rafts, and vines to lash them together. The vines were harder to find—not many of them grew in this acrid climate—but they'd managed to gather enough tonight. Enough to please Peras.

"Come on," Peter said. "We've got plenty. Time to head back."

"Will Peras think it's enough?" Orrin asked. "You remember what he was like two nights ago."

Peter had been confused by Peras's rage that night. It had seemed so out of character. But there *was* urgency. They had to get the rafts built before the Gul'nog came looking for their hideout.

"We've got twice as many vines as we did that night," Peter said, his head held as high as he could manage. "You have nothing to worry about."

"Because if he—"

"Nothing to worry about. Come on. Grab those sticks, and we'll be off home."

"Home," Orrin said glumly. "Home is Aedyn, Peter, not some foul-smelling cave."

"Then let's hurry, and we'll be there soon enough." Peter stooped and filled his arms with a load of branches and draping vines. He almost stumbled under the weight, but righted himself and took a deep breath. "Feels good to be hunting for something other than mushrooms," he said with a laugh.

Which reminded him that the dried meat Peras had supplied was a welcome change over mushrooms, but it hadn't exactly been what he expected. No matter. Why should they waste time getting more interesting food when there was such a rush to get away from this place? They could feast in Aedyn.

They headed back in the direction of the cave, trailing twigs and bits of leaves as they went. The going was slow in the darkness. Even though the Gul'nog seemed to have abandoned their hunt, no one was fool enough to leave the safety of the cave in daylight.

Peter tried to engage Orrin in conversation several times, but all Orrin would do was grunt. Peter was irritated at his silence—his spirits were high, and there were a thousand things to discuss: how the rafts would be built, when they would leave, how Peras would manage to navigate the treacherous waters back to Aedyn. He disliked walking in silence like this now that they didn't really need to.

They were still a quarter mile away from the cave's entrance when they heard the screams. The shrieks of many people. Peter and Orrin looked at each other, dropped the branches, and sprinted toward the sound.

Stumbling in the dark and going too fast to dodge the ends of branches, they tore through the underbrush to get to their home. Heaving with exertion, they stopped in the last shadows before the cliff face. Orrin grabbed Peter's shirt sleeve and dragged him down into the bushes.

Peter almost cried out. The Gul'nog had found them at last. It looked as though they had smashed in the walls of the tunnels—smashed their fists through solid rock—in order to widen it. The narrow passageway hadn't saved them after all. The creatures swarmed in and out of the people's fortress, a pile of rubble at their feet.

The people ran about, pursued by the hulking monsters. In the dim moonlight, Peter could just distinguish the figures—there was Alyce with her five-year-old son, Alexander, clutched tightly in her arms. And there was Gregory, his good hand clutching his opposite shoulder. And there was Matthias, one leg curiously bent and dragging behind the other. Where, Peter wondered urgently, was Peras? He should be here. He should…

His mind froze. There—Lord of Hosts preserve them all—was Julia.

She was fleeing for the safety of the trees, a small bundle clutched tightly in her hand and a Gul'nog in hot pursuit. She was running as fast as she could, but her sprinting was no match for the stride of the monster behind her. It was upon her in a moment. Its fist slashed through the air and connected with her head.

She collapsed without a sound, falling to the forest floor and lying there, unmoving, among the dirt and rocks.

Peter wanted to scream—wanted to run to her side—wanted to kill the Gul'nog with his bare hands, but he didn't need the pressure of Orrin's fingers on his arm to tell him that he had to stay hidden. He kept his eyes on his sister, willing her to move, to show any sign of life, biting his lip until blood came.

The Gul'nog bent and scooped up the small parcel that Julia had been carrying. Peter couldn't see what it was, but the Gul'nog seemed overjoyed with its find. It took the horn that was dangling from a cord around its neck, raised it to its mouth, and blew a long, low note.

It was a sound Peter recognized—he had heard it once before, that night when the Gul'nog had suddenly turned and left him and Gregory alone.

As it had on that other night, the horn gave some signal to the others. The Gul'nog seemed to raise their heads and retreat as one. Suddenly, the cave entrance was empty of the monstrous creatures. The pounding of their feet echoed through the forest as they withdrew to the west.

Peter rushed to his sister's side. The ground was littered with bruised and groaning bodies. His friends lay there moaning, clutching broken limbs, but he stumbled around them, hardly sparing a thought for anyone but Julia.

She lay where the Gul'nog had left her, her arm skewed at an awkward angle under her chest. As Peter reached out to touch her head he could feel a warm, sticky liquid pooling beneath his fingers.

"Julia," he said, his whispers urgent. "*Julia!*"

She moved her head slowly—once, twice, and blinked her eyes open. She focused on Peter just for a moment, and then her eyelids slid closed again.

"Julia!"

"Let her sleep," said a voice, low and soft in his ear. Peter looked up with a start.

It was Louisa. A thin, dark line snaked its way across her cheek, and the hem of her skirts was in shreds almost to the knee. She reached out a hand to touch Julia's forehead, letting her fingers trail through her hair. "Let her sleep now."

Peter nodded, forcing down the lump that seemed to have lodged itself in his throat. "What happened?"

"They came," Louisa said simply. "Peras told the monsters where we were hiding, and they came to find us."

Peter almost laughed. "That's ridic—"

"Peras betrayed us." Her voice wasn't angry. More like tired. "I told you he would, Peter, remember?" She turned her eyes to the front of their cave. "The Gul'nog smashed through solid rock to find us. The rocks began to rumble, and part of the roof fell in toward the back. Everyone was running and screaming, and no one knew where to go. The monsters found them before they could get away."

"Who?" asked Peter, choking out the word. "Who didn't get away?"

"Most of us." Louisa's eyes shut, and she rocked back and forth as she recited the litany of names. "Leon. Alexandra. Simeon. Celeste. Frederick. Elmira. Geoffrey. Carmine."

She continued, but Peter's mind stopped registering after thirty or more names. A gasp escaped his lips, and tears sprang unbidden to his eyes. Louisa named boys and girls, old men and women. Most of the people he had promised to protect.

But he shook his head. This was not the time to mourn. Tears were not scientific. Crying wouldn't bring back the dead, and there was work to do. Rafts to build. And now, though it pained him to do this kind of mathematics, they would have fewer rafts to build, and they could leave this cursed island even sooner.

A gleam in the darkness caught his eye. He reached down and pulled up a short knife. It looked like the one Gregory had used on the mushrooms in the forest. He would return it to him. For now, he just tucked it into his belt and stood.

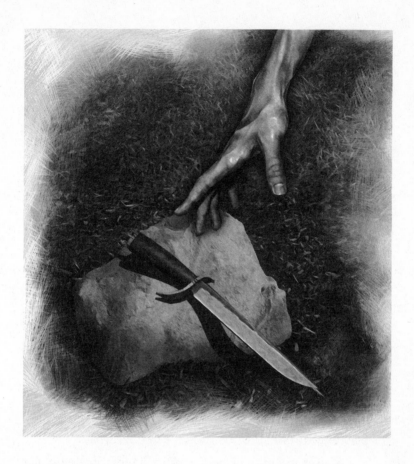

"Peras," Peter said. "Peras will know what to do. I'll find him."

"Peras." Louisa spit out the word as if it were a foul taste in her mouth. "Peras has been lying to you from the beginning, Peter. If he's a true messenger of the Lord of Hosts, why did it take him so long to appear? Why did the Gul'nog seem to abandon the hunt the day he arrived? Why did he arrive the day after the Gul'nog found you in the forest? How did the Gul'nog find our hiding place without so much as a search? They came straight to it. And why, stepbrother, did Peras choose that precise moment to be away?"

She shook her head. "This isn't an ordinary evil, Peter. This isn't a Shadow you can flee from. You can run away to Aedyn and pretend it doesn't exist. But it will come there. It's time to stand up and fight." She stared at Peter with wide eyes, her gaze boring deep into him.

His eyes slid away from hers and he jumped to his feet. "I'm going to go find Peras. He'll know what to do. Take care of Julia."

Louisa watched him go as he ran off into the night. Peter would not believe her yet. And Julia—she touched her stepsister's forehead once more—needed rest.

She stood and looked around. Many of the people from Aedyn had fallen near the rubble at the entrance to the cave. Others had collapsed near the trees. Some were moving, crawling about looking for their family members. Many, like Julia, lay still. But unlike Julia, most would not get up again.

Louisa closed her eyes and took a deep breath, sucking the air into her lungs. She remembered the light that had come to her that day, just before the eruption—

remembered how she had been called. And so she went to work.

She went first to the ones who were in pain—those who were crying out to the Lord of Hosts for his help. She moved among them slowly, one at a time, ripping makeshift bandages from her skirts or from their own clothes to press against wounds. As she touched the people, their cries grew fewer, and their courage rekindled.

And then she came to a face she knew better than the others—a face that had welcomed her at the very beginning.

"Alyce," Louisa said, "you're hurt." Alyce's foot was twisted beneath her at a strange angle, and even under the Shadow, Louisa could see that her face had gone absolutely white. She seemed to be whispering something, and Louisa bent closer to hear.

"Al ... Alexander ..."

Her son. Where was her son? Alyce never let him leave her side.

Alyce reached out to grab Louisa's hand, her nails digging into the skin of her palm. "He was with me ... I was holding him ..."

"I'll find him," Louisa said. "I'll find him for you." She knelt by Alyce's feet and reached out a cool hand to touch her ankle. It was already starting to swell. "I'll sing you a song," she told Alyce. "I need you to rest here, and when you wake, Alexander will be here."

Alyce's eyes were already closed as she nodded.

Louisa hummed a thread of a tune first, and then began to sing in a still, quiet voice:

The two come together; the two become one
With union comes power, control over all
Flooded by light, the shadow outdone,
The host shall return; the darkness shall fall.

Alyce was asleep by the time she finished.

Louisa stood and surveyed the scene, her eyes desperate for the sight of one small child. If he'd been with Alyce during the raid, he couldn't have gotten far. He wouldn't be in the rubble ... he must have run away. But why would he leave his mother? Would the Gul'nog have taken him as a —

Louisa felt someone tugging on the shreds that remained of her skirts. She looked down and saw the small, grubby boy, five years of age, his eyes wide. Louisa bent and picked him up. "Alexander! We've been looking for you." She held him tightly against her.

"I was hiding," he said. "Mother got hurt, and the monster was coming."

"Clever boy," Louisa said gently. "Mother has just hurt her foot, but she'll be all right soon. She's sleeping now."

Alexander nodded, his cheek pressed against Louisa's shoulder.

"And now I need you to be very brave," Louisa said. "We have to find the people who are hurt the worst and get them back inside the cave. It will be dangerous for them to stay out here too long."

"But what if the monsters come back?" Alexander asked, his eyes wide as he looked up at her.

"They won't," said a new voice behind her.

It was Orrin, come from amidst the trees. "Not tonight," he said. "And we'll look for a new hiding place tomorrow. Peter's gone off to seek Peras," he said to Louisa. "Let's help the rest of these poor souls back inside."

It didn't take them long to do so. Alexander ran ahead of the others, calling out his friends' names as he found them, and Louisa and Orrin carried the wounded inside together. It was perhaps an hour before they had everyone safely inside. Those who were less hurt began to tend the weak.

"More patients for you, Healer," Orrin said with a smile.

Louisa grinned and squinted at the sky beyond the rubble that had been their tunnel. It would be dawn before they knew it, and Peter and Peras were still out in the woods. What would Peras do to Peter when they encountered each other? She turned back to the wounded. It was these people who needed her care now.

She went to Julia's side first. The blood had clotted and dried in her hair, and as Louisa took her hand she began to rouse from her slumber. She blinked her eyes open and looked at her stepsister as if she were an absolute stranger.

"Peter," she said. "Is Peter all right?"

"He's out looking for Peras," Louisa said. "You remember what happened?"

"The Gul'nog came," Julia said. "And we couldn't fight back."

"But it won't be that way for long," Louisa said. "We're going to bring the battle to the Shadow, Julia. It won't defeat us—it *won't*! You and me—we'll show the Gul'nog that the people of Aedyn can still stand up. We'll show them that the people of the Lord of Hosts have a power they can never match!"

Julia gave a hint of a smile, and then put a hand to her cheek with a groan. "Don't try to move much yet," Louisa said. "You've got a beastly head wound."

"I was trying to run from … I had … Oh no." Julia sat up, wincing as she did so. She felt the ground around her as if searching for some lost object.

"What is it? What are you looking for?"

"The talisman!" Julia said with another groan. "I'd taken it out of Peter's hiding place when we first heard the Gul'nog coming. I had it in my hands!"

"You didn't have anything with you when we found you," Louisa said, puzzled. "I would have noticed it."

"You would've seen it for sure," Julia said. "It glows blue." She winced. "That wretched creature must have stolen it. Blast it all … Peter will be furious when he hears. Oh, why didn't I just leave it where it was?"

Louisa's face fell. The talisman. "Because if you had, the Gul'nog would've killed us all until they found it. By taking it outside, you actually saved us."

Julia didn't seem comforted by those words. "Well," she said, "I suppose we'll just have to steal it back. And *then* we'll stand up to the Shadow."

CHAPTER

5

Peter crashed through the trees, heedless of the noise he was making. The Gul'nog had gone off west, and he was heading east. Besides, they wouldn't much care about him anyway. They had already done their night's work.

He didn't dare call out for Peras, but then he didn't need to. He knew precisely where he would be: down at the beaches, scoping out their launch site and the supplies they'd assembled. It wasn't much farther, and even in the dark he knew the way.

He was breathing hard by the time he reached the sea. Unlike the lush beaches of Aedyn, this shoreline was stony and barren. Waves lapped darkly at the rocks, and the wind whipped around Peter's head. Here, at least, he could breathe free air. Here, the acrid smell seemed to have burned away.

Peter doubled over, pressing his palms to his knees and gulping in deep breaths of the wind. Even in the cool air he was sweating, and now that he'd stopped running he could feel every muscle screaming, feel the hundred scratches from twigs and branches that had cut his arms and legs as he'd run. But after a moment he straightened and looked around him, realizing he was utterly and completely alone.

Where was Peras?

Peter scanned the shoreline, looking for Peras's familiar figure. He was nowhere to be found. Peter cupped his hands around his mouth and called out Peras's name—not too loudly, for there was no need to take risks. But there was no answer.

After a moment, Peter collapsed on a rock, his chin falling into his hands. If Peras wasn't here—if he wasn't scoping out their launch site—then where on earth could he be?

Did it mean Louisa had been right?

He shook his head. Of course it didn't mean that. She'd been raving when she'd said those things about Peras. It was the tension of the Gul'nog attack that had her speaking like that. Peras must be here somewhere— or else he'd passed him in the woods.

Yes, of course, that was it. He'd been in such a hurry to get to the shore he hadn't noticed Peras in the darkness. Stupid of him, really. And now he really ought to get back and help Louisa at the cave—see how Julia was getting on. Peras would have returned there by now, and everyone would be looking for him.

Peter stood and looked back the way he'd come. The woods were awfully dark. He would have given anything to see the sun again, to run under a bright blue sky. But for now they lived under the Shadow.

Not much longer, though. Soon they'd be in Aedyn, and the Shadow would never touch them there. With that happy thought in his mind and a smile stretched across his lips, Peter went back into the woods in the direction of the cave, swinging his arms as he went.

The journey back seemed quicker—amazing what a good attitude will do for you! He even whistled a bit when he came to the part of the path that always worried him most—the part that skirted along the edge of a cliff. And it wasn't long at all before he found himself back at the cave's entrance.

Julia and all the others were gone. Louisa must have taken them inside. Bodies still lay around, bodies of people he knew. They would have to begin burying them right away. He scrambled over the rocks and into the cave. But the scene laid out before him was not what he had expected.

Peras had indeed returned to the cave. He stood in front of the entrance, a few of the raft men by his side. But he didn't seem to be organizing the wounded or preparing the people to begin burying the dead or working on the rafts. He was standing in front of Louisa, his long arms on his hips, and his face empty of that jocular smile that had always been so comforting. And Louisa was facing him as if ready for an attack.

Peter felt the tension in the cavern and almost couldn't force himself to break into it. "What's going on?"

Louisa's head whipped toward him. "You're back. Good."

Peras turned and, seeing Peter standing there, offered a hand to help him over the last of the rubble.

"Where were you?" Peter asked. "I couldn't find you at the beach."

"We must have missed each other in the woods," Peras said.

Peter nodded. Just as he'd suspected then. Nothing to worry about, and Louisa's mad ravings could be put to rest.

"I wish you'd been here, though," Peter said. "If you'd been here, you could have prevented the whole thing. I would've liked to see that."

Peras raised an eyebrow. "Would I have prevented it? Your 'healer' here seems to think I organized the attack."

Louisa said not a word. Her hands remained
planted firmly on her hips.

Peter thought he hadn't seen her looking so determined since the day she'd cut all the ribbons off Julia's
birthday dress. But this was a new Louisa. He forced out
a laugh, which sounded harsher than he had intended.
"You know girls and their foolish ideas."

Louisa looked shocked, but Peras seemed pleased. "Exactly. Well said, Peter. Now come," he said, putting a hand on Peter's shoulder, "I must have a word with you."

Peter resisted gently. "Sure, but first ... where's Julia?"

"I'm here." Julia's voice came from behind his stepsister.

Peter stepped around both Louisa and Peras to where his sister was lying on the ground, her threadbare blanket evidently having been lost in the attack. There was more color in her face now, a new brightness in her eyes, and Peter grinned at the sight of her.

"Louisa won't let me stand up yet," she said.

"Don't worry," Peter said. "You'll be ready before the rafts are. And then you can rest all the way to Aedyn. By the time we get there, you'll—"

He was interrupted by a cough that came from behind him. Peter turned to face Peras.

The golden-haired savior pulled him aside. "We can't risk it, Peter. We can't take them all."

"What?"

"It's too dangerous. Getting them all through the woods—remember that cliff, now—and then a week's voyage over a sea that will be rough this time of year, on rafts that will be just barely seaworthy, made from scraps of wood and vine ... It's too much, Peter. Most of them would never make it."

"But there's barely thirty of us now. And ten of us will be captains. Surely we can get twenty more aboard." Peter looked around at the ragtag collection of people in the cave. Most had bandages wrapped around a limb. Some were coughing, others moaning. All were desperately hungry. He locked eyes with Gregory, whose face wore a steely expression, his arm hung limply at his side, the sling gone. Peter remembered his willingness to abandon Gregory in the woods. "We can't leave anyone, Peras."

"We'll return for them later, Peter," Peras said, placing a reassuring arm around Peter's shoulder and turning him away. "We'll sail to Aedyn, find weapons, build a great warship, and come back in victory to take them home with us then."

"Well ...," Peter said. Something felt strange about this conversation, but he couldn't put his finger on it. "I suppose it would help if they didn't have to be moved just yet. They could use the time to heal."

"Quite right," Peras said. "Very sensible of you. We have to wait until they're stronger."

Peter felt a dull ache in his head. "But we can't leave them here in the rubble. The Gul'nog will return. We should move them first."

"There's no time, Peter! We must work nonstop to build the rafts and set sail before the Gul'nog return."

"But—"

Peras muscled Peter farther away from the group. "Look at them, Peter. They're weak. Invalids. Next to worthless." He spoke low into Peter's ear. "They're not going to get stronger. Look around you. They've no food, no medicine, no bandages—no hope at all. It's time to save ourselves, Peter. You and me and a few of the others. We can still make it to Aedyn."

Peter felt himself nodding. "Yes, build the rafts. Quickly. Must get away. It's all for the best. Very sensible." He pasted a smile on his face and avoided looking at anyone, avoided Gregory. "Very sensible indeed."

CHAPTER

6

"Did you see him? Did you *see* him? Did you hear what he said?" Julia pounded her feet against the rocky floor of the cave as she paced back and forth in front of the entrance. "'The sensible thing,' he said. Sensible to leave us all here to die!"

Louisa didn't lift her head from her work. She was systematically tearing strips of cloth off a moth-eaten blanket and wrapping them tightly around Alyce's swollen ankle. "Peter's just forgotten," she said, her teeth clenched as she tore a new strip.

"Forgotten *what?*"

"That love is stronger than reason." The strip complete, Louisa worked it underneath Alyce's foot and drew the two ends together. She looked up at Julia and her gaze softened. "Don't worry," she said. "He'll remember."

Julia muttered something about the absolute uselessness of brothers.

Louisa finished her work on Alyce's ankle. "There," she said, tying the final knot with a dramatic flourish. "Good as new. Well ...," she laughed, as Alyce unsuccessfully tried to flex her foot, "it *will* be good as new. Just give it time."

"Time," Julia said with a grumble. "The one thing we have plenty of. Time to sit and wait to die."

"Nonsense," Louisa said. "Honestly, if you're going to take that sort of attitude, you'd best go hunt for mushrooms or find something else useful to do. We have work to do here."

"What sort of work?"

"You mean besides laying our dead to rest? Why, get that talisman back and defeat the Shadow, silly." Louisa raised an eyebrow and cocked her head to the side. "Mother may have been right. You *are* a little dense sometimes."

Julia scowled, but Louisa just gave a laugh that was full of mirth, not cruelty. When she next spoke, her voice was raised, and she addressed the small crowd of people in the cavern.

"Did you hear that? We have work to do!" Thirty pairs of eyes—all that were left of the people of

Aedyn—lifted to her beaming face. "During the attack, the Gul'nog took the talisman of the Lord of Hosts. We've got to get it back."

Julia, who was really trying very hard not to say something nasty and Peter-ish, had to at least question Louisa's plan. "It didn't save us the first time," she said. "What possible use can it be now?"

"It will light our way." Louisa spoke with such certainty that Julia fell silent, resolving to save her protests for later. "We will certainly need it," Louisa said, "in the volcano."

Julia gasped. The faces of the people around her had drained of color, and a storm of objection rose around her.

Louisa held up a hand, and after a moment the murmurs fell silent. "We must go into the volcano," she said, "for it is there that the Shadow lives, and it is there that the Lord of Hosts will assist us in its defeat. There, at its source." She looked around, perhaps expecting cheers, but received only crestfallen stares. "Or," she continued slowly, "we can run. We can turn from the Shadow and try to flee before it. We can look for a place where it won't find us and hope it goes away on its own. That is the choice we make today. Do we run, or do we stand?"

There were cheers this time, though perhaps not as enthusiastic as Louisa might have wished. Still, Louisa smiled like they'd just elected her to Parliament. Her grin was contagious, and Julia broke into a smile herself.

Louisa held up a hand for silence once more. "To business," she said. "In order to get that talisman back, we'll need to learn everything we can about the Gul'nog. Their habits, their movements, their weapons, where they make camp. Everything." She nodded toward Gregory. "You can help us there. We'll need a scout, and you already have experience with the creatures."

"Not experience I'd care to repeat," he said, with a nervous laugh. "But I accept."

"You'll be safe," Louisa said. "We'll all be safe. Never forget: we are under the protection of the Lord of Hosts. He'll keep watch over us even under the Shadow."

Julia wanted to join Louisa in her optimism but couldn't do it. Judging from some of the faces around her, she was not alone in this.

"Safe?" Imogene asked, disbelief in her voice. "Not one hour ago those monsters came and tore through the solid rock wall of our cave. They killed my Simeon and my Elmira. Why didn't the Lord of Hosts keep us safe then?"

Others in the crowd nodded, though no one else spoke up. Julia found herself agreeing with Imogene — and at the same time ashamed that she could so quickly lose faith in the Lord of Hosts.

"And if we weren't safe here when we were hiding and minding our own business," Imogene said, her voice getting stronger, "what makes you think we'll be 'safe' if we march into their camp or into that volcano?"

Now some in the crowd did voice their agreement. Julia wondered if Louisa might have a rebellion on her hands.

But Louisa didn't look worried. If anything, she seemed even calmer than before. "I do not know if all of us will survive. I do not know if any of us will survive."

This got a round of grumbles from the group.

"But the Lord of Hosts has promised me that He will make sure the Shadow is defeated—if we obey His call. We were attacked because we were heeding the voice of a servant of the Shadow. Now we will move forward to do as the Lord of Hosts commands. And doing His will may not always be safe, but it is the only way the battle can be won."

CHAPTER

7

Peter and the others followed Peras to the beach. It was still night, but the moonlight shining off the whitecaps gave enough light for them to see their work.

"And now," Peras said, "we build our rafts. With only the eleven of us, we will need to build only three. Peter, direct the men to bring out ten of the largest logs from our stash. Carry them to the beach here and lay them out parallel to one another. Orrin, you and one other bring out all the vines and lay them here at my feet."

And so they commenced building their fleet. Peter still felt strange about the plan to leave everyone

behind, but Peras's logic seemed sound. And Peter was
the last person to doubt good logic.

It didn't take Julia and Gregory long to get organized.
They were to head out as scouts for the first trip. Their
mission was simply to find the Gul'nog base. Their task
was nothing more ambitious than that. Others would
research their movements and vulnerabilities after the
base was found. It could take them all night to find the
creatures, and no one wanted to risk being caught out in
daylight.

"We'll head northeast first." With his good arm,
Gregory had taken a hunk of coal from the fire and
scratched out a rough map of the island on one of the
walls. He'd labeled the cave, the volcano, the cliff, and
a dozen other points in between. Now he scratched a
thick, dark line from the cave to the volcano. "This is the
way they went after the attack. We'll follow their path
as long as we can."

"You won't be able to find tracks in this light,"
Louisa said.

"Don't worry," Gregory said. "The Gul'nog aren't
the only ones who can hunt."

Julia grinned and swung an extra blanket around
her shoulders. It was practically worn through, but it

would offer some protection from the chilly night air. "We'll be on the lookout for more mushrooms."

"Bring home a bushel," Louisa said.

With that, they were off.

The people had managed to clear most of the rubble from outside the cave's entrance, and the bodies had been moved to a nearby spot in the forest, so Julia and Gregory were able to go forward without scrambling over sharp stones or the remains of their friends. Once outside, they headed in the direction they'd watched the Gul'nog go.

It was too dark to see tracks, as Louisa had predicted, but the most casual of observers could not have missed the fact that something big had moved through here—something enormous. The ground had been absolutely pummeled. Saplings had been torn from their roots. The Gul'nog had cut a swath through the forest as they'd left the scene of the attack.

Julia choked down a gasp as she saw what they'd done. Gregory looked over with a smile. He was trying to encourage her, she knew, but she couldn't stop the feeling of sinking dread that had settled in the pit of her stomach. How could they possibly fight against these monsters and hope to win?

She took a deep breath and thought of the dark lords of Aedyn: the Jackal, the Leopard, and the Wolf. They, too, had seemed invincible. But they had proved no match for the power of the Lord of Hosts.

Would the Lord of Hosts protect them this time, though? That was the key question. As Julia walked silently beside Gregory, she thought back over her adventures in Aedyn. When she'd come here the first time, she'd found herself speaking with a voice she didn't recognize. Words she hadn't thought to say came out of her mouth. She'd screamed, and three horsemen had been knocked to the ground. Later, she and Peter had screamed, and the walls of the stockade holding the children of Aedyn captive had come crashing down.

She knew one thing for certain: if she got in trouble again, she was going to scream.

The thought made her steps feel lighter. Why hadn't she thought of this "scream of power" before now? Maybe that was what the Lord of Hosts was waiting on — someone to scream in faith that He would act. Hopefully, she wouldn't find herself in any situation that might make her feel the need to scream, but if she did, she was going to let one loose.

She and Gregory had one advantage, at least: the Gul'nog were certainly easy to follow. The going was easy too — there were no trees to duck around, no branches left to swing into their faces. And there was no possibility of getting lost, not as long as they kept to the path.

Oh, the path! Maybe, if they were trying to keep out of sight, the path was not the best place to be walking.

She put a hand out to Gregory's arm—his wounded arm, she realized as she saw him flinch. She mouthed an apology and nodded toward the side of the path. He seemed to understand, and still without speaking, they moved off the path and into the trees.

Julia could tell they were near the volcano. The ground seemed softer under her feet and the air grew ever more sulfurous. The dark cloud stretched overhead like an ocean wave about to crash down and drown them.

It was a good thing they'd gotten into the forest when they did, for it wasn't much longer before they reached the Gul'nog camp.

It would have been too dark to see at all, but the Gul'nog were crouched in groups around massive bonfires that lit up the whole space around them. They were at the very base of the volcano, its greedy throat open and still glowing just behind the monsters. The heat from the bonfires poured into the sky, and Julia could feel herself sweating beneath the extra blanket she wore. She looked up at Gregory and saw that tears had come into his eyes.

She knew why. It was hopeless. Simply and absolutely hopeless. Just one of these creatures would be enough to wipe out the small band of survivors they had left, and here were hundreds—*hundreds*—of these monsters. It could not be done, and it was absurd to think any differently. It bothered her to realize that Peter, who had seen the logic in fleeing, had been right all along.

Gregory seemed to be reaching the same conclusion, for he grabbed Julia's hand and took a step back. He didn't need to tell her to be quiet—not for all the world would she have uttered so much as a sound. They backed up slowly, inch by inch, step by careful step, keeping their eyes always on those great bonfires and the monsters who sat around them.

Then Julia stopped.

She squeezed Gregory's hand and nodded toward the fires. He pulled at her arm, urging her to keep moving, but she held fast. With her other hand, she reached out and pointed. Gregory followed her gaze. Julia hoped he would see what she had seen—and would understand what it could mean for the people of Aedyn.

At the outer edge of one of the fires, not fifty yards from where they were hiding, one of the Gul'nog was standing up. Slung around one of its meaty shoulders was a cord, on the end of which dangled an ivory horn. The horn that had called the Gul'nog to retreat. If they could get that horn—if they could use it to draw the monsters away from the volcano—then they could search for the talisman without needing to worry about being discovered. If they drew the creatures far enough away, perhaps Julia and Gregory could bring Louisa and the others here, and they could get into the volcano and

fight the Shadow—all without needing to do battle with its minions.

Julia's mind sped, trying to work out how to get to that horn without being seen. Maybe the monster who carried it would take it off. If it would set it down for just a moment, maybe Julia could snatch it away. But as she stood watching, that seemed more and more unlikely. The horn seemed to be a symbol of power. No Gul'nog would ever willingly remove it.

Gregory jerked his chin back toward the way they had come, and they retreated just far enough that they could whisper without the risk of being overheard.

"We ought to head back," he said in Julia's ear. "We've found the camp. That's all we were supposed to do. Now we regroup and make a plan. Orrin and Priscilla will go out next. They'll track their movements and find a time for us to take the talisman."

"But if we can get the horn, maybe we can use it to draw them away," Julia said "Maybe they'd leave the talisman just sitting there, and we could get it."

Gregory shook his head quickly. "Too risky, Julia. Too many 'ifs.' Let's just go back and report what we've seen."

"But what if this is our only chance?" Julia's whisper was as insistent as she could make it. "We've got to try for it now. We might never see that horn again!"

"*Try for it?* Don't be absurd, Julia. We'd be seen — we'd be caught — and Lord of Hosts preserve us if that happens."

Julia shook her head, her eyebrows knit together. "We'll wait," she said. "We've always thought they sleep during the day. Louisa knows our mission might take until morning. We'll just wait here through the night."

Gregory looked at her as if she were crazy. "They're sure to leave a watch. It isn't safe, and with so few of us left we can't afford to take foolish chances like this. We ought to return and plan with the others. It's what we'd expect them to do if we were the ones waiting back at the cave."

He was right. There was nothing to say to this, yet still Julia stayed where she was, feet planted firmly on the ground. "That's true," she finally said, "but I'm going to stay and try to get that horn. You go back and explain what I'm doing. Tell Louisa you couldn't convince me because I was being 'beastly.' She'll understand." Julia turned her head to look back at the camp. "We don't know what will happen tomorrow, and if Louisa's right, we have even less time than we have people."

She stepped away into the dense underbrush and found a place to lie down and wait.

A moment later, Gregory knelt down near her. "We'll, I'm certainly not leaving you here alone."

Julia smiled. And so they waited.

"When we get out past the breakers," Peras said, "we will lash the three rafts together. This will give us more stability in the waves and will make sure we don't get separated."

Peter approved of this logic. It agreed with what he knew of nautical science. What he wished he could have more of right then, though, was the science of fire. He stood knee-deep in the frigid waves, as he and the other men held onto the rafts and prepared to launch them into the outgoing tide. Oh, for some kind of heated boots right about now.

It would be dawn soon, and Peter's muscles ached from the backbreaking work they'd done all night to get the rafts ready. His mind was so tired from figuring it all out that he would've fallen asleep right then and there if it weren't for the icy water. He figured he needed to give just one more round of strength to help get his raft out beyond where the waves got white and turned over. They'd lash the rafts together and turn everything over to Peras. Then he could curl up in the sun—the beautiful sun that he hadn't seen in two months—and sleep for a whole day if he wanted.

Orrin looked at him from the other side of the raft. They were both at the front, which meant they'd be getting wet first. But it was where the leaders should be. Peter grinned at Orrin with what he hoped was a courageous smile. Orrin's returned smile looked a bit green—and they weren't even floating yet. Peter made sure the little knife he had found was firmly tucked in his belt, and he took a strong grip on the raft.

"After the next wave, men," Peras said. He stood at the back of the third raft, a bundle of vines in his hands. "And … now!"

Peter and the others shoved their raft into the surf, feeling the previous wave withdrawing around them, helping them. Until the next wave slammed into them. Peter was able to hold onto the raft, but Orrin lost his grip. Around them, men kicked and flailed and tried to keep the rafts heading out to sea.

A frigid, exhausting seven minutes later, they escaped the breakers. Peter nodded his head at Peras's good judgment. He was right: there was no way they could've gotten the old women and the children and the wounded through the surf like that. Better to wait until they could all travel on a proper ship. Peter guided his raft to where the other two were already being lashed together.

"Good work, men!" Peras tossed vines to the men on Peter's raft, and they began tying them to the other two. Peras looked heroic even dripping wet. The peach-colored sky of predawn lit him like a superhuman. "It's smooth sailing now," he said. "Who wants dried meat?"

Most of the men were shivering too much to seem interested in food. But Peter raised his hand, and Peras tossed him a stick of the tough meat. It beat mushrooms and nuts, but he did wonder when they were going to see how the Lord of Hosts provided for His children.

Thinking about mushrooms made him think about Julia. "I wonder how the others are doing." He wasn't sure if he'd said it aloud or just thought it. Neither Orrin nor any of the others responded. The only sound was the sloshing of the waves between the logs of the rafts. No one answered, Peter must have just thought the question to himself, but then he saw Peras's face.

The look on their savior's face was dark and angry. Peter was instantly reminded of the night they'd come back without enough logs and vines. How quickly his fury could appear. But what had caused it this time?

"You'd rather go back?" It seemed Peras had barely whispered, though Peter heard it clearly over the surf.

Heads popped up on the rafts as the others looked around to see what was happening.

Peter realized the question was for him. "Um, no. Not until we can build our boat and get them all."

Peras's glare was intense. "That's good, Peter. I wouldn't want to think you were questioning a messenger of the Lord of Hosts."

"Me? Never. How could they have all gone through a launch like that if ten strong men could barely do it?"

This seemed to appease Peras. His muscles began to unclench. "Exactly."

"No, you've been very logical about it all. Very scientific." Peter tore off a bite of the dried meat as if to prove his appreciation for what Peras had done for them. "I was just wondering, though," he said, while chomping the chewy bite, "about my sister. She was unconscious when we left. Some of the others were—"

"Enough!" The anger was back in Peras's eyes, and Peter half-wondered if he was going to walk across the rafts and throw him overboard. "Silence your doubts, unbeliever!"

Now Peras did step toward Peter. The men pulled their legs and bodies out of the way as Peras stalked across the rafts. He stood over Peter and bent down. Peter thought he was going to yell in his face, but instead he grabbed Peter by the shoulder and hoisted him into the air.

"Peras!" Orrin said. "What are you doing? Just put him d—"

"Silence, insect, or you'll be next." Peras turned his furious eyes on Peter, dangling him above his head. "You would question my wisdom, toad? You would question reason and *science*?"

"No!" Peter said, now more concerned about how his arm was getting pulled out of its socket than having a conversation. "Of course not. I lov—*Ow!* I love science. It's my favorite. Nothing wrong with science when looked at correctly. I've built my life arou—"

Peras dropped him so hard the raft almost tipped over. "Good. See that you remember that." He stepped back toward his raft. "See that all of you remember!" He shouted it to the sea, his arms stretched wide. "Defy me, and find yourself swimming home."

Peter rubbed his shoulder. Orrin crawled over to see if he could help, but Peter shook his head. He looked over at the far raft. Peras had changed. Or perhaps he'd been like this all along, and Peter had just refused to see it. He looked down at his little knife and vowed to have it ready if Peras ever came at him like that again. But would it do any good? He looked again at the muscular brute with the golden hair. If this was a messenger of the Lord of Hosts, something was terribly wrong.

For the first time since Peras stepped into their cave, Peter was afraid.

"Beastly animals."

Julia shook her head as she watched the Gul'nog finish their savage feast. The hiding place she shared with Gregory was over fifty meters away, but she could see their violent ways well enough from it. And with the sun finally starting to rise over the horizon, she could see the violence even better.

She didn't know what kind of animals the Gul'nog had eaten. Some kind of deer, mostly, along with rabbits, and even possibly some owls or hawks and a pig. The monsters didn't seem to care, so long as it was red meat. She hadn't seen them eat any humans, but she imagined they would love it.

Perhaps you've never known the feeling of being something's future meal. When you've gone to a zoo or have been out on an exploration, maybe you have seen the hungry look in the eyes of a lion or bear or wolf or shark. People live their lives thinking they are the top of the food chain, that if they had to they could eat just about any kind of animal if it meant staying alive. But when you are being looked upon as nothing more than a meaty meal, it reminds you that people are not the kings of the universe.

The Gul'nog hadn't even cooked their meat, though there were bonfires all around. Judging from how they'd fought among themselves for the last animal left alive, it was *the fresher, the better* for them.

Julia noticed that the sky had begun lightening. She marveled at the changes, the first time she had seen the light of daybreak in two months. Now, as the dawn's rays poked through the trees into their filthy camp, the monsters appeared to get sleepy. They licked the last bones clean, belched, and tossed the bones into the fire. There must be some kind of pecking order, Julia thought. They kicked and thumped each other to get the shadiest spots and settled down to sleep.

Julia looked over at Gregory. He'd managed to sleep, lucky bloke. She pushed his shoulder, and he awoke with a start.

"What? Are they attacking?"

"Shh! No, we're fine." Julia came to her knees to look over the fallen log they were hiding behind. Gregory sat up. "It's like we thought," she said. "They're going to sleep just as the sun comes up."

Gregory stretched his good arm and yawned. "Did you sleep?"

She looked at him as if to say, *You have to ask?*

"Oh," he said. "Sorry. I guess I could've watched some and let you sleep."

"No matter. I wouldn't have anyway."

He rubbed his injured shoulder and patted down his hair. "So where's our musician?"

"I'm sorry?"

"Our horn player," he said. "The giant with the pipes."

Julia got it. "Oh. Well, he's the big boss, apparently, so he got the best spot. They only have one hut in the whole camp, and that's his. He went in with half a rabbit about thirty minutes ago, and he hasn't come out."

Gregory gathered his feet beneath him as if to stand. "Well, let's get to it then."

"Wait!" Julia grabbed his wrist. "They've posted two guards, one at each end of camp. The closest is right … there, just coming out from behind that fire that's almost out."

Gregory looked to where she was pointing. "Um, scrawny runt—for a Gul'nog. Must've lost the battle to see who had to take first watch."

Julia hadn't noticed that before, but he seemed to be right. Compared to the others, this guard was just a pup. Of course, a short giant is still a giant. She thought he was probably seven feet tall at least. More than a match for both of them combined.

"So what's your plan?" Gregory asked.

She'd been hoping he'd ask that. "The plan is for you to stay here while I sneak in and get the horn. Then we go back to camp, get everyone ready while it's still daylight, and come back and lead the monsters away with a toot."

Gregory looked at her as if waiting for her to say something else.

She felt herself blushing. "What?"

"I'm waiting for the end of the joke, of course."

Now she was mad. "I'm not joking. That's the plan, take it or leave it."

He raised his hands. "Leave it! Did you get a bad mushroom? Julia, that's not a plan, that's crazy talk. You'll be caught for sure."

"I will not. Look, our closer guard isn't even pretending to patrol around the camp anymore. Now that everyone's asleep, he'll probably find a shady spot and sack out himself."

"Probably? *Probably* and *maybe* and *if* are going to get you served up as a Gul'nog appetizer."

She ignored him. "You can't do it because you're a big oaf with a bad arm. You'd trip over something and wake up the whole camp."

He looked like he was going to object, so she went on quickly.

"I'm small and smart and fast. I'll zoom from spot to spot quick as a breeze and be back out here with the horn before you can say 'Bob's your uncle.'"

He blinked at her. "Who's Bob?"

"Ugh, never mind! You just stay here, and I'll—"

Gregory gripped Julia's shoulder tightly but not unkindly. "Are you absolutely certain you want to do this, Julia? Now that we know they sleep during the day, we can come back here in a few hours with everyone. We can make our grab then. And if it works or it doesn't work, it won't matter, because you can lead them away from the group either way."

He turned to look back into the forest. "There are plenty of good hiding places here. So the group can be in these trees. And whether the whole camp wakes up and chases you or whether you blow the horn and they follow, either way the rest of us will sneak around behind and get to the volcano. We'll just ..." He turned back around. "Julia?"

She was already twenty meters inside the Gul'nog camp.

Julia saw him notice her. Despite the danger she was in, she almost laughed. It was sweet how worried he was about her. Even from this distance, she could see the concern on his face. She thought for a minute he would

come running after her, but thankfully he just settled
back into their hiding place to watch.

To watch her succeed, she hoped, not to watch
her come to a gruesome end.

She remembered she was going to scream if she
got into trouble. That scream of power. As she crawled
between two sleeping Gul'nog—their snores almost as
disgusting as their stench—she wondered if she'd actually be able to scream or if she'd be too scared when
they were about to catch her. She held her breath and
crawled on. She'd just have to make sure it didn't come
to that.

Julia snuck behind a pile of firewood. The horn-
blower's shack was another fifteen meters away. She cast
a glance toward the nearer guard. He hadn't sat down
to sleep yet, but he wasn't patrolling either. He was
standing at the top of the cliff overlooking the ocean.
He appeared to be examining the sea or the black
shadow from the volcano. No matter—his back was to
her. She turned back toward the hut. There were just
... she swatted a fly away ... eight Gul'nog to get past
before ... another fly landed on her nose, and she shooed
it away ... before she could get to the entrance of the—

What *was* it with all the flies?

She looked around the stack of wood and saw
what it was. A carcass of a large bird—an eagle, perhaps—lay on the ground in a sprawl of feathers, legs,

and gnawed meat. She thought it was a raven at first, so many black flies were on it. A puff of wind from the sea shook them all to flight, revealing the brown feathers beneath. Then, just as quickly, they were on it again. Julia thought she was going to throw up.

She thought briefly of Louisa's request for them to bring home a bushel of mushrooms. Not likely. Judging from how desecrated and filthy this camp was, even fungus wouldn't grow here. And the sight of that poor bird had chased her appetite away at any rate.

Her eyes now caught the motion of swarming insects from all around her. From all over the camp, in fact. A feast for flies. The bugs seemed to land mostly on the carcasses, but they also seemed to like the Gul'nog and other unidentified piles of ... something ... all over the ground just as well. Getting caught because she threw up too loudly—now that was a danger she'd not anticipated when she'd made this plan.

But whether it was from the night of gorging or the morning sun, the nasty creatures around her seemed sound asleep. She glanced at the near guard and observed that he'd sat down to look at the ocean now. She spotted the far guard pacing away out of sight. Then she crawled as quickly as she could toward the horn-blower's hut. She could've gone even faster, but she couldn't make herself get too near the piles of goo.

The boss's shack wasn't much more than a three-log teepee with wolf pelts pinned up as walls. A deerskin pelt hung across the opening as a sort of door. Keeping herself hidden between a weapons rack and the side of the shack, she slithered up to the entrance and peeked underneath the deerskin.

The inside was surprisingly dark. She had to wait a few seconds for her eyes to adjust. In the meantime, her nose and ears told her all she needed to know: there was a stinky Gul'nog in here, and it was fast asleep.

When she could finally see a little, she found the inside of the hut to be basically a penned-in version of the exterior of the camp. Nasty piles of goo, half-eaten carcasses covered with buzzing flies, a small fire pit, and a sleeping giant snoring away.

Was she really going to go in there? She looked back toward Gregory, but couldn't see him from here. Across the camp, the Gul'nog remained asleep. But it was an eerie calm, like a room in which dozens of people were hiding and were just about to jump out and yell "Surprise!" Still, there was nothing to tell Julia she was in any extra danger right now.

So she readied a scream in her throat and crawled inside the hut.

CHAPTER

8

"What do you say, Peter—some breakfast for you?"

Peter looked up at Peras. The sun was over the horizon now and directly behind Peras's head. His golden hair, shimmering in the light, still gave him the look of an angel, but his face was in shadow. His eyes nothing more than glints of black stone.

Peras held another strip of dried meat toward Peter. "Well?"

Peter took it. "Thanks." He took a bite off the stick, and Peras moved on. Dried meat again. Wonderful. It wasn't as if he expected Peras to be able to serve him crumpets and tea in the middle of the ocean, but he'd just expected more from a servant of the Lord of Hosts.

As Peras pulled another meat stick from his bag and extended it toward one of the men on the middle raft, a wave tilted the boat, nearly knocking Peras into the water.

Peras caught himself on the tiller and mumbled a word that, if Peter hadn't known better, would've sounded almost like a curse. Peras tossed the bag to the middle of the raft and sat down like a sulking child.

Something about how he did it was odd to Peter. So human. It made him see Peras in a new light. What did it mean to be a servant of the Lord of Hosts? Peras had said he'd been traveling to the island ever since the talisman had been activated. Peter had been thinking that meant Peras had left, well, wherever servants of the Lord of Hosts lived, and traveled undeterred through any obstacles that came his way in order to reach them, possibly traveling through the cosmos themselves. Which meant he'd been thinking of Peras almost as an angel.

But it all felt wrong now. What kind of angel falls over on a raft? What kind of angel gets mad at people for not getting enough sticks—or for thinking of their sister's well-being? Would an angel really get embarrassed and curl up in a corner? What would he do next, suck his thumb?

A frightening thought began to form in Peter's mind. So frightening that he wouldn't let it come together. Not yet. He packed it down and concentrated on the men lying around the three rafts.

Most of them were already getting sunburned. At least half had fallen asleep after their long night of work, but Orrin and a few others were awake and munching on chewy dried meat.

Fifteen-year-old Mitchell, their youngest crewman, crawled over to Peras's bag and dug through it. He pulled out three meat sticks. Then he rummaged around inside it some more. He seemed to explore every pocket and fold. Finally he upended the bag over the raft and shook.

Nothing came out.

Peter sat up. What was this?

Trevor, their oldest crewman, slid over to Mitchell and took the bag from him. He shook it and dumped it too, then cast it aside. He and Mitchell—and Peter—cast their eyes around the craft, as if more bags of food might've magically appeared just now.

Trevor met Peter's gaze. He saw the message there: we've no more food.

As Peter was deciding whether or not he wanted to risk another choking, Mitchell beat him to it.

"Eh, Peras," the teenager said.

Peras grunted but didn't look at them.

"We, well ... I was wondering," Mitchell said, "what we're going to eat after these three strips are gone."

Peras swung around and assessed the situation. "You went through my bag?" He stood up meanacingly, his legs spread wide. "How dare you?"

"It's a fair question," Trevor said, his voice quivering with age and perhaps something else.

Peras stepped across from his raft to the middle one and reached down as if to pick Mitchell up by the throat. Mitchell fell on his rear and backed away. Peter crawled forward, his hand going to the knife in his belt.

Trevor moved between Peras and Mitchell and raised a bony finger at him. "Leave the boy alone."

Peras seemed lost in his anger, like an enraged bull determined to charge. But he shook his golden locks and seemed to relax. He straightened his posture. "Careful, old man, or we'll solve our food shortage real easily." He picked up the food bag and snatched the three meat sticks from Mitchell. He waved them in front of Trevor. "But I guess all you'd make for us would be more dried meat."

The whole crew was awake now. Peter looked around to see if anyone else thought Peras had meant they would start eating each other to stay alive. From their looks of concern and anger, it appeared most of them had.

"What about it?" Peras asked, his arms held out as if to take on any challengers. "Anyone else want to challenge the servant of the Lord of Hosts?" He met every man's stare, one by one, but no one would hold his gaze. Peras scoffed. "I didn't think so."

Mitchell seemed close to tears. "But what are we going to do for foo—"

Peras spun around and tossed the last three meat sticks out far across the waves. "For food, I can snap my fingers, and fish will jump out of the ocean and into your laps. Quail will fall from the sky and onto your plates." He brought his finger into Mitchell's face, and neither Trevor nor Peter could get there in time. "I'm making the decisions on this voyage, boy. You got that?"

Mitchell whimpered and nodded. Trevor and Peter pulled Mitchell back behind them and stared at Peras defiantly.

"Relax, men," Peter addressed the group without taking his eyes off Peras. "I'm sure our messenger from the Lord of Hosts has a plan. Don't you, Peras? We all know you haven't brought us out here simply to die— or to leave our wounded and our women and children unprotected. Right?"

Though the only sounds were the play of the waves on the rafts and the gentle *whoosh* of the sea breeze, even those seemed to grow quieter as everyone watched Peras and waited for his answer.

Peras seemed almost unsettled by this display of rebellion. But then his jaw clenched and he looked over them all with anger. "The next one to challenge my leadership will be food for someone. If not for us, then for the fish."

Peter felt himself thinking that if they all rushed him at once, they could overpower him. But he quickly put the idea away. How could they overpower an angel? Even if he wasn't an angel, he was as strong as a Gul'nog and nearly as big. It would be a foolish attempt.

Peter saw the men looking around uncertainly. Many of them looked from Peras to Peter, and then away. They weren't ready to attack either. Maybe they wouldn't ever be. Peter sank back on his rear, and the moment passed.

Peras sniffed at them with disgust and went back to his raft. The others sat or lay down again. More than one looked out longingly in the direction the last meat sticks had been thrown. Maybe the waves would bring them back to the boat.

The meat stick in Peter's hand had only a couple of bites taken from it. He was suddenly famished, and it seemed as though he wanted nothing more than a holiday feast of the chewy meat strips. But if this was the last food he was going to get—maybe ever—he had to make it last. He rolled it in a strip of cloth from his garment and stuck it under his belt on the side opposite his knife. He pulled a cluster of vines over his head like a stringy umbrella and tried to go to sleep.

The thought he'd felt rising before, the thought he'd stomped down, broke through and played across his mind like a play on a stage. What if Louisa had been right? In his mind's eye, he saw her in the cave standing up to Peras while everyone else cheered.

She'd said he would betray them. Peter hadn't allowed himself to even consider that option, but now that he thought about it, it did seem strange that Peras had "found" them just after the Gul'nog had. And that the Gul'nog had left them alone while Peras was with the survivors, almost as if they were working together, coordinating their actions. Then the Gul'nog had come straight to their hideout without looking. How could they have done that if they hadn't been led there? And why had Peras, their supposed protector, been gone when the Gul'nog had attacked?

But no! It couldn't be. Peter looked over at Peras. He stood straight and strong, a master of the sea. Surely that man could not be working with scum like the Gul'nog. Even if he weren't an angel from the Lord of Hosts, why would a human betray other humans?

Besides, he thought with a zing, there was the thing with the talisman. He and Julia had activated it in secret. No one had seen them do it—except perhaps the shadowy form that had erupted from the volcano far away. Surely only the Lord of Hosts could've seen or even known about it. When Peras had come to their cave—*directly* to their cave, he recalled—he'd known about the talisman being activated. How could he have found their cave? The Gul'nog hadn't known where it was exactly. And how could he have known about the talisman if he weren't from the Lord of Hosts?

It was too much for Peter's mind to handle without some rest. So with his eyes on the dark shadowy cloud now consuming the morning sun, and with his mind on Louisa and Julia, he tried to go to sleep.

CHAPTER

9

The Gul'nog boss was intimidating even in sleep. Julia dropped the deerskin flap behind her and studied the creature before her.

Even in the near-darkness, she could see that its skin was barely on the brown side of green. Its shoulders and muscles were enormous. Its nose was too wide and poked forward into a rounded point. Rotted teeth peeked out between black lips every time the creature exhaled a snore.

Unlike most of the other Gul'nog she had seen, this one wore bits of armor. A strip of hardened leather with metal spikes draped each hip, and a cruel-looking plate with spikes the length of Julia's foot was strapped to its right shoulder by a cord of old animal gut. The head and front legs of the rabbit it had brought in here to eat hung off one of these spikes.

It took nearly a minute for Julia to overcome her revulsion and fear of the monster slumbering in front of her. As she gathered her courage, her eyes never left the other item decorating the beast.

The horn.

Its strap wrapped around the Gul'nog's neck. The horn itself lay under its arm like a little girl sleeping with a baby doll. No, wrong image. Like a wolf sleeping with a chew toy.

The horn seemed to be made of real horn, like from a steer or something. Julia again almost threw up thinking about putting her mouth where this filthy beast's mouth had been. Still, her whole plan revolved around getting this thing, and she'd risked so much getting this far, so she might as well do it.

She quietly rolled to her feet and crouched before the creature. Then, as if trying to pluck something out of a fire without getting burned, she stretched her right hand toward the cord.

Ew, she thought, but she made herself keep inching forward. Her fingers shook as they came within the Gul'nog's body space, then under its chin.

As if picking up a dead bug, Julia pinched the cord between her finger and thumb. Gently, she lifted it toward the creature's ear to pull it over its head. The

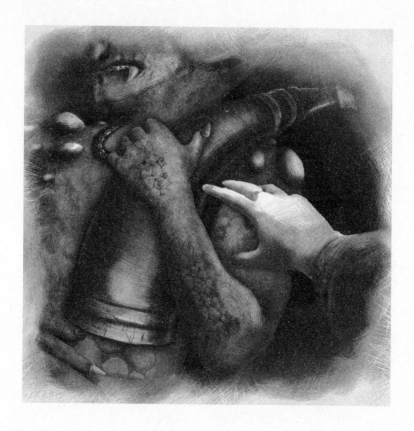

thing exhaled, and she felt its hot breath and spittle on the back of her hand. She almost bolted out of the hut then and there, but somehow she kept herself where she was. She had to bring her other hand up to help, which meant turning her whole body to face the creature's head.

You can do this, Julia. You can do this.

She spread her hands apart on the cord, lifting one loop over the horn-blower's ear and the other over its chin and nose. This was going to work. She was almost there.

Julia kept her eyes on her right hand to be sure the cord didn't brush the beast's eyes or forehead. But that meant she wasn't concentrating as much on the left hand, and the cord rubbed against the scalp of th—

"Hnng!" the Gul'nog grunted.

All of Julia's plans—to fight, to run, to scream— and all of her bravery flew out the top of her head like a fly off a dead animal. *She was going to die!* Julia tried to make herself run, but she was paralyzed. Her body didn't obey her mind, and her mind was going crazy.

But after the thing's grunt, it didn't eat her. It didn't even open its eyes or roar out for the others to come running. Instead, it snorted, smacked its lips, and did the next worst thing beside having her for dinner.

It rolled over. Onto the cord.

Oh … beetle juice!

Julia's heart pounded so hard it didn't feel like it was in her chest anymore but was thumping its way up her neck. Every second that passed was another second closer to discovery. How she'd gotten away with this so far was a miracle. Why had she come up with this stupid plan? Why hadn't Gregory stopped her?

Okay, Julia, calm down. You can still do this.

Right. Julia took a deep breath and moved slowly around the Gul'nog's feet to the other side.

The horn was actually in a better place now. The thing's arm wasn't cradling it anymore. But the cord had gotten tangled around the spikes on the Gul'nog's shoulder armor. If she had ten minutes and no giant lying on it, she could probably yank it free. But now?

She looked at the remains of the rabbit. Poor thing. That would be her if she didn't get this horn and get out of here.

An idea struck her. What she needed was a knife. Surely this beast had one on him somewhere. She thought of the weapons rack outside. One of those huge spears would be a bit much, but it would at least have a sharp—

Wait. There on the ground she spotted what looked like a broken ax blade. Whether it had broken off because of being used to hack through too many trees or too many bones, she didn't know, but it would do.

She sneaked over to the corner of the hut and lifted it from the dirt. Even broken off and only the size of her hand, it was still heavy.

Julia held it over the creature's head. She had a brief notion to slam the blade into its neck or something. Killing it in its sleep would be what an assassin would do. But knowing her luck, she'd barely break the skin, and it would wake up and bite off her head.

So she went back to the first plan, which was to use the blade to cut the cord.

She knelt at the Gul'nog's head and licked her lips. This would be delicate work. She couldn't pull very hard on the cord to cut it, or the other end would pull into the monster's neck and wake it up.

Carefully, she picked up the cord from where it lay across the shoulder armor. She thought at first to cut it loose from the spikes and then pull the cord out from under the beast. But now that she looked at the situation, she decided the better idea would be just to cut the horn loose from the cord altogether.

She lifted one side of the horn and brought the blade down. *Snip.*

Goodness, that blade was sharp. She thought she'd have to saw it back and forth, but the cord had severed like a cooked noodle on a fork.

Snip. The horn was free. She held it in her hands as if it were made of solid gold.

No time for that now, though. She tucked it into the folds of her garment and headed for the door.

As she lifted the bottom corner of deerskin and felt the first breeze of "fresh" air on her face, she realized she'd been holding her breath a lot in the hut. Almost free now. Only fifty meters of sleeping Gul'nog and two guards to get past.

She looked over the camp to find the guards. As she did, she realized it had gone strangely dark outside. Was a storm coming? It was still early morning, so how could it be ... Oh. The Shadow. The black cloud from the volcano had covered most of the sky, and now it had eaten the sun. She remembered the day of the eruption and how the Shadow had seemed to be not just a cloud of ash and rock but somehow alive. A creature. She shook her head. Louisa wanted to defeat the Shadow. But how can you defeat something that blankets the sky and eats the sun?

She spotted the near guard. It was asleep now, atop the cliff where it had been gazing at the ocean. The dark sky must have helped it feel comfortable enough to drop off to sleep right where it sat. She couldn't be sure about the other guard. She thought she saw its head and shoulders off beyond one of the smoldering bonfires, but if so, it wasn't patrolling anymore either. That was good news for her.

With a quick prayer to the Lord of Hosts, she cupped the ax blade in her hand and crawled through the deerskin and behind the weapons rack.

From here, she could see the trees where she hoped Gregory was still waiting. She even gave a little wave to let him know she was okay. Now to get over there.

Slowly, she crawled back toward the woodpile where she'd first hidden. The goo piles and decaying carcasses were still there, but something about the darker sky made them seem less awful. *Slightly* less awful. The flies seemed fewer as well.

A light caught her eye. At first, her mind told her it was just the embers of a bonfire, but something had been different. She scanned the camp in the direction she'd seen the light. Hadn't it been … blue?

There! Another thirty meters away, not toward either guard but not toward Gregory either, she saw the blue flash again. A pile of stones as tall as a dog sat in a small clearing surrounded by at least eight sleeping Gul'nog.

That blue light … it couldn't be.

But of course it could be. These Gul'nog had stolen it from her very hands, hadn't they? At the thought of that night, her head wound throbbed again, though it was mostly healed.

The talisman. Could it be here?

Now that she thought about it, she was surprised it hadn't been in the boss's hut. Or maybe it was there and she'd missed it, and this light was just something else.

The idea of going back into that hut was too much. She couldn't put herself through that again. As she sat there thinking, she felt how exposed she was. If Gregory were watching her, he'd be beside himself with worry wondering why she was just sitting there.

She looked closely at the light. There was no denying that something was there, buried under the stones. And wouldn't it make sense that they would bury it under rocks and surround it by guards?

With the realization that she was probably going to regret it, Julia started off toward the blue light.

After ten meters of crawling, with the ax blade chafing her wrist and the horn about to fall out of her clothes, Julia decided to risk standing up to a crouch. She immediately felt better and moved faster. More stealthily too. And without the bright sunlight, she didn't even have to worry about her shadow passing over a Gul'nog's face and waking it up.

In fifty steps she was at the ring of sleeping Gul'nog that surrounded the pile of rocks. The one closest to her was the fattest Gul'nog she'd ever seen. She'd need a running start to jump over that one. So she moved to the next. How they managed to have the discipline to form an unbroken circle and to maintain it even in sleep was beyond her. Maybe they knew what would happen to them if they didn't.

Finally, she found one small enough to step over, and so she did. But was being surrounded by these giants really better than being on the outside? No time to worry about that now.

The rocks in the pile were of that curious lightweight kind formed by ancient volcanoes. The rocks were craggy and pitted, but lighter than any rocks she'd ever lifted. The ax blade in her hand was heavier than half the rocks in the pile.

She set the blade down and began removing rocks carefully. She scraped one against the other, and almost jumped at the sound. Apparently what they lost in weight they more than made up for in noisiness. They all but screeched when touched together. Maybe that was part of the alarm the Gul'nog had created around their treasure.

So she lifted each rock silently off the rock beneath and set them a distance apart from one another in the dirt. They were so light she wanted to move quickly, and the blue light that began beaming out made her want to rush before it shone in a monster's eyes. But she knew that if the rocks came screeching down upon themselves, the whole camp would wake up, and she'd be done for.

One rock off—quietly now … one rock down—not touching any other rock. Another rock off … another rock down.

Finally, she could see for sure what was making the blue light. The talisman! Its six-sided star pendant pressed into the larger amulet from Captain Ceres.

She plucked it off the stack and held it before her. *At last.*

Julia turned toward the trees. Time to quit pressing her luck and get out of here. She reached down to get the ax blade, and the horn slipped out and almost fell to the ground. This was crazy. She left the axe blade in the dirt and drew the horn out of her garment. She would do this with the horn in one hand and the talisman in the other. She went back to the skinnier Gul'nog and stepped one leg over.

And that was when the guard roared.

CHAPTER

10

The second guard! Julia saw it all the way across the camp. It was running toward her at full speed. It passed a weapons rack and pulled a spear off, roaring the whole time.

All around her, the Gul'nog began waking up. Some jumped up, ready to face an attacker. Others sat up more groggily. Either way, Julia's luck had run out.

She bolted for the trees.

A Gul'nog stumbled in front of her, rubbing its eyes. She zoomed past it and hurdled another still on the ground.

She'd gotten halfway to the trees, but her moment of surprise was over. The creatures took up the guard's roar and reached for her. Julia heard the clang of weapons being drawn. She ran as fast as she could.

Ahead, the bushes shook, and Gregory burst out. He held a sturdy-looking tree branch, but he was hardly a threat to the monsters. Still, a couple of them turned toward this new surprise, and Julia got past a few more.

From the corner of her eye she could see the creatures running beside her to catch up. Some ran surprisingly quickly, and she saw that they intended to get in front of her and cut her off.

Only one Gul'nog stood between Julia and the woods now, but it was a big one. It released a roar so frightening, so carnivorous, that she almost passed out from sheer terror. Its jaws unhinged to a monstrous width and revealed lines of saliva stretched over sharp teeth. It lunged for her, and Julia knew she was caught. Its mighty claw grasped her by the head and lifted her up.

Then abruptly dropped her.

The Gul'nog fell over. Along with half of Gregory's branch.

Gregory tossed the other half at the other Gul'nog warriors, who stood trying to figure out what had happened. He yanked Julia's hand—the one with the talisman—and pulled her into a run.

Julia's head was still spinning from the thought that she was about to die. "What … happened? Why did it—wait, you're running the wrong way."

Gregory was leading her not into the trees but beside them. The forest sped by on their left side, and the Gul'nog swarmed toward them on their right. Ahead, the second guard awoke from his napping spot beside the cliff and looked around sleepily.

"I know," Gregory said, huffing with effort. "We'd never get away that way. They're too … fast."

"But where—"

The only thing in front of them was a dead end. The cliff over the ocean stood right before them, with the wide sea beyond. The guard was on his feet now.

"No!" Julia said. "You're crazy!"

"It's the only way!"

She pulled her hand away and stopped. "No, it isn't." She turned to face the Gul'nog chasing them.

The creatures were so surprised at this, they stopped too, with the back ones running into the front ones.

To Julia's left, she saw the boss Gul'nog fly out of his hut in a rage. Apparently, he'd noticed something missing.

It's now or never, Julia.

She turned to the Gul'nog mob and raised her arms to the sides like an opera singer, the horn in one hand and the talisman in the other. She gathered her voice and let loose her very best scream.

The Gul'nog fell before her.

At least, one of them did. Someone had tripped him from behind. The others just stared at her. A few snorted something that sounded like a laugh.

The Gul'nog who had fallen got up and ran toward her. The others charged behind him.

Julia turned and ran.

Gregory stood looking at her. "What was that?"

"Nevermind!" She grabbed his hand, and they ran together toward the cliff. "That should've worked."

Julia wanted to take a minute to stop and see if there was really water below the cliff or just an open jaw of jagged rocks, but she could hear the Gul'nog right at her back. One reached out and narrowly missed her hair.

As she ran, she brought the horn to her lips, monster spit and all, and tried to blow.

Pfft.

Pf—oot.

Pffff.

"Oh, nevermind. Here!" She flipped the horn over her head and hoped the Gul'nog would stop and fight for it and leave them alone.

Judging from the sound of colliding bodies behind her, some had. But if the thumping right at her heels was any indication, not *all* of them had. And to their right, the boss Gul'nog was coming up fast. The guard fell in behind him.

Julia risked a look at Gregory, running beside her. His face said this was possibly the last stupid thing they would ever do.

The cliff's edge was just three meters ahead now. Dried plants clung to the edge next to pebbles and water bird nests.

Two meters now.

Water below still, but *right* below the cliff? Close enough for them to reach it? She couldn't see.

One meter.

The Gul'nog right behind. Were there rocks down there? And, oh, it was much farther down than she—

With one hand clasped in Gregory's and the talisman clasped in the other, Julia threw herself over the cliff.

There were rocks below. Julia saw them as she hurtled down in freefall. Ocean waves crashed against the rocks, sending up plumes of white spray that reached her feet nearly as soon as she'd entered open air. The roar of the surf circled her as if she were falling into a dragon's open mouth.

But it looked like her jump had been just crazy enough and propelled by just enough fear that she had landed beyond the rocks.

She was aware of Gregory falling beside her. And something else. From behind and above her came the sounds of scratching, fumbling, and finally animalistic yelping as at least one Gul'nog tumbled off the cliff as well.

The water and rocks rushed up toward Julia, but she had enough time to realize that she would miss the rocks only to be bombed by a hairy, smelly monst—

Splash.

The water was shockingly cold, but it beat landing on rocks. She gripped the talisman with both hands and kicked sideways—away from the rocks, she hoped—away from the falling Gul—

Splash.

Splash-splash-splash. Splash.

It was raining giants.

Julia kicked to the surface just in time to see another Gul'nog fall into the sea. She caught a glimpse of the creatures beating the water's surface all around her.

Above her on the cliff, scores of Gul'nog looked down, shaking their fists and weapons at her. They jostled each other, and one started to fall. It grabbed for the two beside it, and all three fell. They had not jumped far enough to clear the rocks. As an incoming wave raised Julia's position, she saw them land in a gruesome heap on the boulders.

A strong hand grabbed her arm.

"Aagh!" she screamed.

The hand did not let go. It tugged her and spun her around, though she tried to fight.

"No!" she cried. "I won't die here! I won't!" She yanked her wrist and pulled her feet up to kick the attacker away.

"Julia, wait!" It wasn't a Gul'nog attacking her — it was Gregory helping her.

She stopped fighting.

Gregory had a nasty-looking scratch on his forehead. Blood dripped down onto his right eye, and when a wave crashed over him and washed his face clean, the wound oozed more blood down his face. "Do you still have it?"

"What happened to you?"

"Do you have it?"

"Do I have what? Oh, the talisman. Yes, it's—"

Something long and heavy sliced into the wave beside her. That was no Gul'nog.

"They're throwing spears!" Gregory said, looking up at the cliff. "Come on!" He began swimming away. Not out to sea, exactly, but toward the forested shore about fifty meters away from the cliff.

Another spear came hurtling right toward Julia.

She lurched in the water and lunged back. The spear skewered the water where her head had just been.

"Julia!" Gregory shouted over the sound of the breakers.

It was then that Julia noticed the Gul'nog in the water around her were no longer splashing. In fact, she couldn't see them at all. It made her remember that some of the creatures had seemed to fall, but not bob back up to the surface. Even without armor, they were all muscle and dense bone—maybe they sank like rocks.

Or maybe they were great swimmers and could hold their breath for an hour, and maybe they were right now creeping up under her feet about to pull her down.

With a tiny screech, Julia kicked after Gregory, clutching the talisman in one hand, but using the other arm to make her go faster.

The spears came faster now. They plopped and splashed all around her. And it wasn't only spears but swords and clubs and the occasional thrown Gul'nog. But the beasts appeared to have terrible aim, and nothing touched her.

After five minutes of hard swimming for Julia and Gregory, the Gul'nog either ran out of things to throw or realized it was kind of dumb to toss all their weapons into the ocean, and the deadly rain stopped. The Gul'nog moved around the cliff's edge, following Julia's progress as she swam. But eventually they reached the far edge and had to stop.

She wasn't sure, but Julia thought she saw the Gul'nog leader gesturing and giving orders. Soon the remaining beasts left the edge of the cliff, and Julia couldn't see them anymore. The odds were good that they were even now running around to the forested spot where she and Gregory were going to try to get out.

Julia swam harder.

The waves didn't push her as much here. Instead, she felt an even colder current coming from the direction of the land. A wave swell lifted her high enough to see. The forest ahead was split where a stream entered the sea. That was the source of the cold water, she figured, and it might be the thing that could save them.

No wonder Gregory was swimming this direction. If they could make land there, on the right side of where the stream spilled into the ocean, the Gul'nog would have not only a long way to run from the cliff, but also they'd have to cross the stream. With any luck, there would be no bridges nearby and they'd all stand there at the edge trying to figure out if they wanted to get into the water. That was something they clearly didn't like doing.

Maybe, just maybe, Julia and Gregory would get away.

CHAPTER

11

"Is he out?"

Peter watched Trevor creep over to where Peras was supposedly asleep against one of the oversized logs on the third raft.

Trevor reached forward silently and waved a hand in front of Peras's face. Nothing. He waved again, more broadly this time. Nothing. He looked over at Peter and shrugged.

"All right," Peter said. "Everybody come here, but keep quiet."

The nine men from Aedyn—Orrin, Trevor, Mitchell, and the rest—crept across the three rafts until they encircled Peter on the raft farthest from Peras. The sky overhead was gloomy because of the Shadow. Peter

could see the sun as a feeble brown circle trying unsuccessfully to burn through the dark cloud. The seas had
become rougher over the last half hour, and the rafts
bobbed and creaked together in the turbulence. But
none of it seemed to interrupt Peras's sleep, which was
fine with Peter.

"What are we going to do?" Limas asked.

"Yes," Orrin agreed. "Because if that long-haired
spawn of a Gul'nog is a messenger of the Lord of Hosts,
I'm a twiddlepat hummingbird."

One man snickered. The rest stared stonily at Peter.

"That answers my first question," Peter said. "I
wondered if I was the only one thinking it."

"Did you notice that the current is not carrying
us toward Aedyn?" Trevor asked.

Mitchell looked around as if he hadn't noticed
this. "But he hasn't told us to paddle. I thought the water
would just, I don't know, push us there. By the Lord of
Hosts' magic, maybe."

"You're right," Peter said. "Look, Khemia is still
right there, just as far from us now as it was hours ago."

They all looked. The volcano island was a good
couple of kilometers away, but it was not receding into
the distance. Nor was any other landmass coming into
view ahead of them.

"Should we start paddling?" asked Kelman, a
skinny man with a pockmarked face.

Trevor lifted his hands. "Which direction would we paddle?"

Peter leaned in and spoke in a harsh whisper. "I'm done with this," he said. "I made a mistake. How Peras made me believe we could leave the others behind and come back, well, I don't know. But it was the wrong thing to do."

A gust of wet wind sprayed his face. "I don't know who this *person* is, but I agree with the humming-bird here," he said to Orrin. "Peras is no angel. And if he sleeps, he's no demon either. Which means he's human like us." Peter pulled the short knife from his belt. "I say we jump him, all together and all at once, and tie him up in some vines. We paddle back to land, and we go save the rest of our people."

The others looked at each other uncertainly.

"Are you sunbaked?" Limas said. "That man can lift us up with one hand. You've got a little knife, but what do the rest of us have? It would be suicide." He backed away from Peter. "Forget it. I say we just ride it out and trust that he's really taking us somewhere that we can't see right now."

"Now you're sunbaked, Limas," Trevor said. "We're out of food, and we never had much drinkable water. If we don't get to land soon, it won't matter if Peras is an angel or a … or a—"

"Or a *what*?"

Peras stood over them like an agent of doom. The wind tousled his long blond hair, but he no longer looked angelic. Behind him, the volcano spewed ash into the sky, and the Shadow reached over them like a trap closing in.

"It was him!" Limas shouted, pointing at Peter and backing away. "He's trying to turn them against you. But I defended you!"

"Is that so?" Peras almost smiled. He grabbed Kelman by the hair and held him out over the ocean with one arm. Kelman screeched, but Peras shook him as if holding a kitten by the scruff of its neck. "Planning a little rebellion, are you, Peter?"

The others looked at Peter tentatively, but they all seemed to subtly back away from him.

Peter's pulse pounded in his ears. "Fine." He drew his knife and held it out toward Peras. "Put him down, Peras. This is between you and me."

Peras's eyes grew wide, and he actually laughed. "Look who's got a wittle bitty bwade. Gonna clean under my fingernails, wittle man?"

The tip of Peter's knife dipped. What was he doing? This man might not be superhuman, but he was a lot closer to being superhuman than Peter, a schoolboy from England, was. Peter suddenly felt like he had when his father had screamed at him for being unkind to his stepbrother, stepsister, and stepmother.

The thought struck him like a tidal wave upending the boat. It was as though he were right back in their home on the east coast of England, and Father was shouting at him again. Peter had just gotten sent home from school after getting in the fight with Mason. Peter Grant was a weakling compared to Mason, a problem to the headmaster, and a disgrace to his own father. Peter should show good sportsmanship, Father said. Peter had dishonored the family name, Father said. Peter might as

well crawl away and die, Father said. Or might as well
have said, anyway.

For a trembling instant, Peter wished his mother
were still alive. He *did* feel like a weakling. He wanted
to run and hide himself in her skirts.

But Mother was dead. And Father had turned
into a creature like the Gul'nog. And his stepmother was
Queen of the Underworld whose spawn were Bertrand
the beast and Louisa the … Well, Louisa the healer.

Somehow, thinking of Louisa brought strength
back into Peter's muscles. The tip of the knife rose again.
If Louisa could overcome her natural tendencies and become something better, so could he.

Lord of Hosts, give me strength.

An image of Gaius flashed into Peter's brain. The
old monk stood in his mind's eye, urging him to courage.

Peter gave Peras a calculating look. This was no
angelic warrior. This was nothing more than an overgrown schoolyard bully. A good man once, perhaps. A
father figure who had lost his way. But now he was a
brute, terrorizing the little ones around him.

It was going to stop here. Whether Peter could defeat him or not, it didn't matter. All that mattered now
was that Peter was not going to be a scared child anymore.

"Peras, creature of lies!" Peter said, shocked at the
power in his own voice. "Put him down and face me, if
you're man enough."

For a moment, Peras looked unsure. The waves rocked the boat, and Peras seemed almost to lose his balance.

Then he lifted his head to the Shadow and bellowed. "Very well, I shall kill you first, wittle boy." With a flick of his hand, Peras flung Kelman into the sea. "And we shall all feed on your flesh and drink your blood."

Peter's feet felt bolted to the raft. The only direction that seemed to offer no resistance to him was to jump. He could leap into the ocean and try to make it to land.

But the thought of running sickened him so much that he advanced on Peras instead. He would not embrace his fear.

The distance between them was small, but by the second step Peter was running. He came at Peras in a crouch, his left hand forward as if to grapple and his right hand poised to stab. The last steps of Peter Grant, the boy, and the first stride of Peter Grant, the man.

Peras caught Peter's left wrist.

Peter had been expecting that. He used Peras's own strength to give his strike extra power. He jabbed forward with his right hand, aiming the knife for the heart.

Peras jerked Peter down, but not enough. The blade sunk into his belly, just below the rib cage.

This time, Peras bellowed in surprise, anger, and pain. He became enraged, grabbed Peter by both shoulders, and slammed him to the floor of the raft.

Peter hit so hard he broke through a log and remained wedged there. Black seawater geysered through the hole.

The pain in Peter's lower back was intense, but he didn't care. He would have no second chance. The blade remained lodged in Peras's gut, and he had to get it back.

Though something was wrong with his left shoulder, Peter nevertheless used both arms to pry himself out of the hole in the raft. He rolled out and got to his feet. Was it the sky that had darkened almost to the shade of night, or was it only his vision?

Peter was vaguely aware of the others on the raft. They seemed paralyzed, unable to do anything but watch with fascination. No matter. This wasn't about them.

"Aaaaagh!" Peter shouted, and ran at Peras like a bear. He meant to smash into Peras right where the knife handle protruded—to drive it deeper in and maybe push them both overboard.

But Peras side-slapped Peter's head, sending him spinning to the raft like a swatted fly.

Peter hit the logs but immediately sprang up. He landed on Peras's left side and clung there as if trying to climb a tree.

Peras tried to shake him off, but Peter hung on.

He felt himself slipping, though, so he grabbed the handle of the knife. His first thought was to use it as a peg to hold his weight, but as soon as he grabbed it, it came out, followed by a spout of bright red blood.

With that, Peter fell to the floor of the raft. He spun away from Peras, but the big man was too fast. He caught Peter by the hair and lifted him into the air.

Peter wished his hair would rip out in Peras's hand, but it didn't. It just tore at his scalp with excruciating pain. But Peter wouldn't give Peras the satisfaction of flailing like a fish, as Kelman had.

He stabbed at Peras's arm with the knife. He stabbed and sliced and whittled. Deep cuts sprouted on Peras's arm.

Peras howled. He reared back his left arm and slammed a fist into Peter's ribs.

The world darkened around Peter, and he felt he might pass out. But he couldn't. He couldn't die while unconscious. He had to go out fighting. If Peras wasn't going to let him live, he wasn't going to stop slicing his arm.

Stab, stab, cut, slice, stab.

Another punch came, but Peter wrenched his arm back to partially block it. Though his arm took the blow, his ribs weren't hurt any further.

Slice, cut, stab.

Blood flowed down Peras's arm as if he'd dipped it in red paint. It poured out, dripped off, spattered onto Peter's cheek.

Peras growled inhumanly and lifted Peter's head to his own face. His eyes—once the kindly blue orbs of a savior—had turned black as tar pits, bottomless as the throat of the volcano. The Shadow above seemed to leave the sky and merge with those eyes. Whatever he'd seemed to be before, Peras was now revealed to be a creature of darkness.

"Who dares oppose the Shadow?" Peras cried.

The sky erupted with lightning. It spidered overhead and joined together in cruel white columns. A bolt forked into the ocean, and for a moment the sea turned electric purple. A thunderclap crashed with almost physical force.

Someone screamed from across the waves, and Peter knew something had happened to Limas.

"Bothersome rodent!" Peras shouted, shaking Peter's head and splashing him with blood. "You think you can defy the power of darkness in its finest hour? You will be crushed, and then I will turn on the others. On the children and the old." Peras licked his lips wickedly. "And your women. On your precious Alyce and Louisa and ..." he pressed his nose against Peter's, "Julia. I will roast her alive."

"You … will … not!" Darkness circled Peter's vision. He couldn't pass out. Couldn't. "The Lord … of Hosts … will—"

"Will do nothing!" The sky spangled with lightning again, lighting Peras's face like a madman in a frenzy. "The Lord of Hosts will watch and weep and sit on his hands, an impotent excuse for a god!"

The darkness increased, and this time Peter knew it was only his vision. He was slipping into unconsciousness. Lightning flashed and thunder boomed, but it seemed far away. What Peter needed now was to sleep.

Everything went silent then. It was clear that Peras was shouting something right in Peter's face, but it was as if Peter had gone deaf. The sea roiled and the sky shook and the volcano spewed fire, but it dissolved into muted whispers.

One sound emerged. Isolated from the others. The gentle sluicing of the waves against the rafts and up through the hole in the floor. How peaceful was water. How like a lullaby.

Peter realized his vision had gone sideways. Peras and the others stood on a wall to the right, their heads looking left. The volcano shot ash leftward instead of upward. The others…. They were no longer sitting but were engaged with Peras in a crazed dance on the wall.

Then Peter was alone on the raft. That was nice. A little privacy and rest, at last. In the corner of his mind he heard a voice he knew.

"Peter? Peter, where are you?"

Mother? Mother, I'm here!

Where was she? He looked all around, but all he saw were darkened hallways leading this way and that.

Mother?

"Peter? Peter!"

I'm looking!

"Peter! Wake up!"

A familiar face floated over him. But not Mother's. It was a man. He had a name. Peter knew it, but he couldn't think of it.

The face turned away. "He's coming around."

Peter felt himself being lifted up to a sitting position. The raft was no longer on its side. All was righted.

"Orrin?"

Orrin smiled at him, and the faces of others he recognized pressed in close and smiled too.

Peter blinked at them. It was nice to see them, but he'd been hoping to see his mother. "Why ..." He swallowed. "Why are you all wet?"

That was apparently funny, because they all laughed. Peter would've liked to join them, but he became aware of pain throughout his body. His arm, his ribs, his scalp, his back.

Then he remembered. He sat up as if prodded. "Peras! Where is he?" He tried to get up, but someone held him down.

"It's all right," an old man said. Trevor—that was his name. "We took care of him."

Now Peter thought he must be dreaming after all. "What do you mean?"

Mitchell—that was the teenager's name, Peter felt sure—stood and propped his foot up on something. "He's right here, Peter. But don't worry." Mitchell rolled something over with his foot, and Peter saw it was Peras, bound by vines and looking very small. "He won't bother us anymore."

Peter put his face in his hands and shook his head. "Someone better explain this to me. My head hurts too much to figure it out."

Orrin reached back and pulled someone into Peter's vision. It was a thin man with a pockmarked face and bits of exposed scalp. "It was Kelman here who took up where you left off," Orrin said. "Peras was all, 'I'm the king of the world, you measly humans,' and then Kelman climbed up behind him and socked him in the kidney. Peras was so surprised, he dropped you and went to the ground like a sack of turnips."

Peter looked at Kelman in surprise. "You, Kelman? But you'd been thrown off the boat!"

"Yeah, but I know how to swim," Kelman said. "I swam back to the raft as quickly as I could. I thought I was right as rain, but I hit him in the kidney when I was going for his head. Fell a little short."

Everyone laughed.

"So," Orrin said with a shrug, "when the brute fell, the rest of us saw our chance, and we jumped him. Even Limas joined in despite being zinged by lightning."

Peter gazed at them with new respect. "You men are amazing!"

"We couldn't let you be the only hero, now, could we?" Trevor said.

"I'm no hero," Peter mumbled. "But then, why are all of you wet?"

"Oh, right," Orrin said. "In the scuffle, we all went overboard. Limas was the tipping point. Rushed in with so much force we all tumbled in for a drink."

"Oh, my," Peter said. "But how did you overpower Peras?"

Trevor looked surprised. "Turns out our lumbering friend doesn't like water much. Might not even know how to swim!"

"Cried like a baby, he did," Mitchell said. "'Save me! I'll do anything!'"

Peter tried to imagine it, but couldn't.

"We threatened to let him drown unless he did what we said," Orrin said. "He sat there meek as a lamb as we tied him up and put the gag on him. He's been the model prisoner ever since."

Mitchell prodded Peras with his foot. "Haven't you, little insect?"

Peter tried to get up, but the pain was too great. Orrin and Trevor helped him to his feet. From this vantage, Peter noticed that the seas had become calmer and that the freak lightning storm had passed. The day even looked more like a dim day now, not like a night of doom.

Peter stepped across the rafts, feeling his injuries with every move. He found Peras lying on his side on the raft with the hole in the floor. He lay in a puddle and appeared more concerned with keeping water out of his nose and mouth than conquering the earth. His wounded arm had been wrapped in strips of cloth torn from his own garments. Not that the bandage did much good, seeing as it was soaking wet. The stab hole in his belly had been filled with wadding and wrapped with more cloth, though all of it was stained red now. He gazed up with eyes that had turned blue again, and he seemed weak.

In all, with the bindings and the gag and the bandages, Peras looked to be a defeated enemy. But Peter had been tricked by this man's appearance before.

"I don't know," Peter said. "I'm not sure how wise it is to leave him here. Let's not forget how good

he is at pretending to be one thing while really being
something else."

Mitchell sat against a log and put both feet against
Peras's back. "You think we should just roll him off into
the ocean?"

This seemed to alarm Peras. He struggled and
moaned.

"Stop, Mitchell," Peter said, though he wasn't exactly sure why.

Orrin stood at his shoulder. "It may be the best
way. You're right. He can't be trusted."

Peter's head seemed to clear, and he remembered again that night he and Gregory had searched for
mushrooms—the Gul'nog, how Peter wanted to run.
Would've too, if he hadn't been spotted.

How could he do that? How would he be any different from his enemies—the Gul'nog, or even Peras—
if he did that?

"No," Peter said resolutely. "Mitchell, put your
feet down. We'll not throw him overboard."

Mitchell looked disappointed. "But why?"

"Because we are men, servants of the Lord of
Hosts—not murderous Gul'nog. Besides," Peter said,
heading back across the raft, "he might prove useful."

Mitchell and Orrin grumbled, and the others
looked unsure, but no one contradicted Peter.

"Still," Peter said, "I want six of us watching him at all times. If he chooses to abuse our mercy, *then* you can toss him into the deep."

This seemed to encourage them. Several volunteers moved to surround Peras.

Peter picked up a smaller log that had come loose during the scuffle. "The rest of us, pick up something to use as a paddle. And let's get back to Khemia, where we need to be."

CHAPTER

12

"Why does it glow?"

Julia looked at Gregory as they tramped through the forest, then down at the talisman, which lit their immediate area with a blue light. "I don't know. I don't remember it glowing when we first put the pieces together. Maybe it had to warm up or something." She saw Gregory wince as he pulled a small branch aside. "How's your arm?"

He rubbed it briefly. "It's all right. So long as we don't jump off anymore cliffs or have to swim across the open seas again."

"I didn't want to jump off the cliff in the first place, remember?" She checked behind them. "But I will say you did throw them off our path. Too bad you had to throw *us* off to do it!"

The morning had passed without incident. Their fear of pursuit had all but disappeared.

"How's your cut?" Julia asked.

"Fine," Gregory said, touching the gash over his eye. "Crusty."

They walked together in comfortable silence. They were following a deer path, which meant their feet were mostly clear of brambles or large obstacles, but they had to bend over quite a bit to avoid low-hanging branches and vines. In those places where she could stand upright, Julia had learned to walk with her arm stretched up before her. The spider webs were usually invisible until they were right upon them. It was better to break through one of the sticky nets with her arm than her face, Julia had found. Besides, the thought of spiders crawling through her hair was almost enough to make her scream.

And why hadn't her scream worked? Julia recalled so vividly screaming before and seeing those three horsemen knocked out of their saddles. That was more than just surprise—some force had gone out with that scream and pushed them back. So why hadn't it worked with the Gul'nog at the cliff? She should've been able to scream them into a full retreat, just as she and Peter had screamed down the walls that had held the children prisoner. Had Julia done something wrong? Or was not working just a one-time thing?

Maybe she wasn't Aedyn's Deliverer anymore.

Julia looked at Gregory as he walked behind her. *He* still believed she was chosen by the Lord of Hosts. She smiled sadly. It was amazing how different she felt toward him now compared to how she'd felt just yesterday. They'd been through something together. Too bad she would have to go back to her world one day. Probably one day soon. She would miss him.

"Oh!" Julia stopped mid step.

Gregory turned around. "What is it?"

"I forgot to look for mushrooms, and now we're almost back."

He chuckled. "I don't think Louisa will mind. Not when you hand her that talisman."

Julia fingered the strap she'd rigged so she could carry the talisman around her neck. "I suppose you're right. Besides, I'm sick of mushrooms."

Fifteen minutes later, they emerged into their clearing at the bottom of the cliff face. It didn't appear any more work had been done to clear the rubble from around the cave entrance, but a glance into the forest showed that the others had begun burying the bodies. Julia and Gregory stepped into the clearing just as the sun dipped behind the edge of the Shadow, throwing the scene into gloom.

"Wait," Julia said to Gregory. "I have a bad feeling."

"Nonsense," he said, striding forward. "Everything's fine. You'll s—"

"Halt!" It was a woman's voice, and she sounded deadly serious. The voice came from the cave entrance.

Gregory and Julia held their hands up.

"It's just us," Gregory said. "It's Gregory and Julia."

Julia got ready to run.

Priscilla stepped out from the cave, holding a spear made of a leafy branch with a sharpened end. The young woman looked so tired and thin that she might fall over if she walked into a spider web. But she wasn't a Gul'nog.

"Priscilla," Julia said, "good job challenging us. But we need to go inside. Is everything all right?"

Priscilla seemed to be having trouble concentrating. "Stay … stay back." She jabbed at them listlessly with the branch. Its leaves rustled.

"Now, Priscilla—"

An arm came out from the cave and pulled Pricilla's branch away. "Nonsense," another female voice said. "Priscilla, go get a nap. I've got this."

It was Louisa. She spun Priscilla around and marched her toward the interior of the cave. Louisa turned back and opened her arms to Julia and Gregory.

"What was that about?" Julia asked, as they embraced.

"Oh, nothing," Louisa said, moving from Julia to Gregory for a hug. "We've just been sleeping very little since you two didn't return when we expected. And it's a terrible thing to dig graves for people you knew and cared about. We're all on edge. Inside, they're certain the Gul'nog will return to finish them all off. But we'll be fine now." Her gaze turned serious as she reached for Gregory's face. "What happened to you?"

He pulled her hand away from his eye. "It's all right. But we've had ... an adventure."

"I can see that."

"Louisa," Julia said, "I've got some bad news."

Louisa seemed to brace herself. "You couldn't find the camp?"

"Oh no," Julia said. "We found the camp."

"Then what?"

"We ... we weren't able to find any mushrooms."

Louisa looked from Julia to Gregory, then back to Julia. "That's it? That's your bad news?"

"Yes," Julia said with mock sadness. "You said to come back with a bushel of mushrooms, but all we brought back was this." She pulled the talisman from around her neck and held it toward Louisa.

Louisa squealed so loudly Julia was afraid it might cause a rockslide. Or remind every Gul'nog within a hundred kilometers that they were here. But it did warm her heart to see Louisa so happy.

"Oh!" Louisa said, hugging them again and again. "I can't believe this! We are saved! However did you manage to come by this?"

Julia began to explain, but the others emerged from the cave wondering what was going on. Alyce came out with Alexander. Priscilla came back out, looking half asleep. Imogene was there. In thirty seconds, the entire band of survivors stood around Julia and Gregory, rejoicing over the return of the talisman and basking in its blue glow.

"It's kind of a long story," Julia said. "It's enough to know that we did find the Gul'nog camp. Then we found the talisman. And ... then we jumped off a cliff and swam in the ocean, with spears and things falling all around us."

The crowd looked at them with awe.

"Actually," Gregory said, "it was mostly Julia. When we found their camp, I was ready to return here, but Julia wouldn't have it. You should've seen her. She was unbelievably heroic."

Louisa took Julia by the shoulders. "Unbelievably foolish."

Julia shrugged. "Yes, I thought that a few times along the way. But it was what you needed, wasn't it? And we didn't know if we would ever have the opportunity again."

Gregory coughed. "And there is the slight possibility that there are hundreds of Gul'nog on our trail," he said. "Angry Gul'nog ... but with fewer weapons. Or very wet ones."

This sent a tremor of fear through the group.

"Then there's not a moment to waste," Louisa said. She turned to Julia and Gregory. "Everyone inside, we must prepare."

Julia followed Louisa inside their cave. She was struck again by how much damage the Gul'nog had done—and how few people lived there now. Way over against the far wall she saw her bed and longed to stretch out in it, rocks and all, but there was no time for that now.

Louisa led them to the map of the island Gregory had etched on the wall. She pointed at the volcano. "The Shadow lies here. Now that we have the talisman back, we can defeat it. But we must do so at its source."

Gregory looked around at the women and children and wounded who remained. "But how? If we had an army, perhaps we could do this. But what can *we* do?"

Alyce stepped forward, Alexander's hand in hers. "Yes, we are the weak and the wounded. But we are all that's left, Gregory. And our courage is no less than that of an army."

"But ... what of the ones who died? Surely you haven't finished burying all of them in a day."

Louisa shook her head. "We will trust the Lord of Hosts to care for them until we can return."

Alyce got a knowing look in her eye. She leaned forward boldly and took the talisman from Louisa. She stretched out the cord and placed it around Louisa's neck.

Julia gasped. As soon as the talisman rested on Louisa's chest, it was as if Louisa became someone else. She seemed to stand straighter, and she looked older. Her skin glowed, as if the talisman were shining from inside her.

The others cried out in surprise and joy, and as one they went to their knees.

Julia found herself with them. Could this be Louisa, the impossible stepsister who had followed Julia and Peter out the door to bring them trouble? Before her now stood—not a petulant brat—but the one thing they had all thought Peras was.

Louisa was the messenger of the Lord of Hosts.

He had answered their prayer before they had known what to pray for. And He had transformed a heart in the process.

Louisa, healer and deliverer, walked among the people. "Don't kneel before me," she said, touching each person on the head. As she did, Julia saw each person's face relax. Louisa touched Gregory's face, and it was as though the deep gash above his eye was only a spot

of dirt that Louisa wiped away with her finger. A thrill
went through the group.

When Louisa touched Julia's head, Julia felt as
though she were a young girl again, nestled in her father's arms. He had been so kind then. Before. As Louisa
passed to the next person, Julia caught a glimpse of the
talisman. One large piece and a star-shaped hole. When
they'd first seen it, the hole had been empty. Then Julia
had found the missing piece and had placed it where it
belonged.

Could she do that with her own father? His heart was missing some piece. He'd lost it when Mother had died. Could Julia somehow fill that hole?

"Stand, all of you," Louisa said.

The survivors of Aedyn stood. But to Julia's eyes they were no longer the small and broken. They were no longer even simply survivors. They stood strong and tall and ready to storm the very gates of the underworld. These were no wounded and weak. These were the warriors of the Lord of Hosts. He had his army now, and they would march on the enemy.

"The light will lead us!" Louisa said.

As she said it, a light sprang out from the talisman and shone in the cavern like a bright white flame. All the fatigue washed out of Julia—and all the hunger was replaced by a pleasant fullness similar to the one she always got after eating Christmas dinner. She felt as if she could march right up the side of the volcano, jump in with a cup of water, and vanquish the fire.

Without another word, Louisa led everyone outside their cave again. They stepped over the rubble as though it were the ruins of Jericho, and their faith in the Lord of Hosts had brought down stone walls.

Light flooded the clearing. It was still afternoon, but it might've been noon on a sheet of arctic ice for how brightly it shone. Louisa stepped resolutely toward the volcano, and the nineteen others fell in behind, shielding their eyes from the unaccustomed brightness. The light traveled with them, surrounding them like a shield. It no longer seemed to emanate from the talisman, but from all around.

As Julia walked, marching along in step with Louisa, she thought she could almost hear parade music playing. Here they went, striding to victory. She looked up at Louisa—stepsister, friend, and heroine—and smiled. The look Louisa gave back told Julia that come what may, the battle was theirs.

"Wait!"

Julia looked off to her left, toward the sea. The group had been walking in the light for more than twenty minutes, but she felt she could continue walking forever.

Over a ridge and upon a wooded slope, she saw Peter and the others from the rafts. "Peter!" she cried.

The men came running forward, then faltered and raised their hands against the glare of the light around Louisa's warrior walkers.

"It's all right!" Julia called. "It's the power of the Lord of Hosts. You're safe." To Julia, Peter and the men looked exhausted but confident. She almost thought they *had* built a new ship and were here to take them home. But someone was missing. "Where's Peras?"

Peter and the others approached the group. Several had warm reunions with people in Louisa's group.

Peter seemed to be moving with difficulty, as if he were in pain. He gave Julia a gentle hug. "Hey, sis. It's good to see you."

"Took you long enough," she said. "But Peter, where's Peras?"

He looked over his shoulder. Julia saw Mitchell and Kelman come over the ridge with Peras walking between them. The large man was bound at the hands, feet, and mouth. He shuffled along in baby steps. His long, blonde hair was stringy and matted. His clothes were in tatters, and he had bloody bandages on his right arm and around his middle.

"What on earth did you do to him?" Julia asked.

Peter walked to Louisa and looked like he might give her a hug, but instead he extended a hand as if shaking hands with a fellow scientist. "Louisa was right all along. We got out on the water, and Peras turned into … Well, if I described what his eyes did, you wouldn't believe me. I'm still looking for a rational explanation for it all. But we discovered one thing for sure. He is not a servant of the Lord of Hosts."

Julia beamed at Louisa. "We know. *She* is."

Peter looked at Louisa with wonder. "What?"

Louisa smiled humbly. "It's a long story. I'm just glad you saw the truth about Peras before any of you were seriously hurt. Though I see several wounds among you. Let me look at you, Peter."

For the next fifteen minutes, the group rested on the forest turf in the bright light of the talisman as Louisa saw to every injury. Julia saw Alexander, Alyce's son, following Louisa as she made her rounds. Louisa smiled at the boy often and seemed to be instructing him. She would whisper to him, and then they'd go to an injured man and touch him near his wound. Julia saw more than one look of amazement as something happened in the wounded men. Louisa would smile and give Alexander a hug and a word or two, and they'd move to the next man.

At last, Louisa came to Peras. Julia and Peter went over, as did nearly everyone else. They clustered around as Louisa and Peras squared off once more.

"Well, Pretender," Louisa said, "I see you have done what I could not."

The gag was still on Peras's mouth. His expression remained hard, but questioning.

"I tried to tell these people that you were a traitor and blackguard," Louisa said. "But they wouldn't listen. It is said that a tree is known by the fruit it produces. I see you couldn't maintain your illusion for very long at all. I'm only glad they saw through you before you were able to work your treachery."

Louisa reached forward, and Peras flinched away as if expecting to be struck. But she merely laid her hand on his right arm. Julia wasn't sure she liked what she saw, but it was clear from Peras's face what she had done. He moved his arm back and forth and around as much as the bindings allowed. Judging from his manner, Louisa had healed him. She touched his belly wound next, and he had the same reaction.

Peras stood as if stunned, looking at Louisa with wide eyes. Whether he was thinking she was an idiot to heal her enemy or thinking something else altogether, Julia couldn't tell. She only knew that *she* would probably not have healed him. A glance at Peter's face made her think he wouldn't have either.

Alexander looked from Peras to Louisa. "Healer," he said, "why did you help him? If you make him stronger, won't he just try to hurt us again?"

Louisa smiled mysteriously and winked at Alexander. She lifted her head to the group. "We've a battle to fight, men and women of the Lord of Hosts. Come, let us advance on the enemy."

With that, she turned and strode toward the volcano. Julia and Peter and the others followed, and the light traveled with them.

CHAPTER

13

"Were there this many in the camp?" Peter looked over the battle line of Gul'nog standing between them and the active volcano.

Julia wagged her head. "A few more in the camp, I think. They lost a few at the cliff."

Peter and Orrin looked at each other in amazement. Peter whistled. "Julia, I take back everything I ever said about girls being cowards."

Gregory grunted. "You should've seen her."

It was early evening now, and the setting sun had again broken through the Shadow near the horizon. This had the curious effect of making it brighter now than it had been at noon. Nevertheless, the shadows were long behind Louisa's little army—and longer still behind the Gul'nog force that stood a hundred meters before them.

The people from Aedyn stood on a wide plain that led gradually up to the base of the volcano, which even now sent roiling clouds of gray ash into the sky and dumped burning rivers of lava down its slopes. The Gul'nog battle line was over a hundred strong. They had apparently either found more weapons or made them, because every Gul'nog was armed. And it didn't look like the sunlight was bothering them in the least.

The light from the talisman was as strong as ever, but Peter didn't feel as shielded now as he had in the dark forest. He looked at his fellow rafters and the other men, women, and children of Aedyn. It didn't take a theoretical physicist to predict the outcome of a battle. Of course, ever since he'd come to this strange land, he'd begun to see that there just might be something beyond the laws of science and reason.

Trevor, the old man from the raft, pulled Peter aside. "Remember what you said about our hostage proving himself useful?"

Peter looked at Peras, who was still bound and gagged and held by Mitchell and Kelman. Peter smiled back at Trevor. "Exactly what I was thinking."

For the tenth time since they'd emerged from the forest and seen the Gul'nog waiting for them, Peter reached for the knife on his belt. It was still gone. He'd lost it in the fight with Peras and had forgotten to look for it until they'd gotten on land. By then it was no-where to be found. It had probably gone overboard in the scuffle.

So Peter settled for trying to sound tough. He walked to Peras and gave him a little shove forward. "Send them back."

Peras, Mitchell, and Kelman looked at Peter un-certainly.

Peter glanced over at Louisa, who nodded. He pulled the gag from Peras's mouth and began working on the bindings around his arms. "Waddle out there, get their attention, and send them back. Or we will finish what we started on the raft."

With the gag off and his arms free, Peras looked menacing again. His eyes didn't go black, but they nar-rowed. "Even now, in the presence of the Shadow, you think you can escape destruction?"

Kelman yanked Peras's hair. Peter thought the gesture was too harsh, but then he remembered how both he and Kelman had been jerked around by Peras in the same way. Still, Peter didn't like copying a tactic he despised.

"All right," Peras said, probably wondering how much damage he could do with his arms free but his legs bound. "But it's going to take more than a bright light to save you today."

Peras took a baby step toward the Gul'nog lines, but at that very moment the creatures let out an inhuman shout and charged forward. They raised their weapons and galloped forward like a tsunami of muscle and hate.

The creatures kept coming, despite Peras's shouts and waving arms. When they were fifty meters away, Peter could make out the crazed eyes and slobbering jowls of each one. He saw an especially large one in the middle, leading the charge, wearing spiked armor, and brandishing a white horn in one hand and a cruel-looking sword in the other. Peter recognized this Gul'nog from the raid at the cave.

Peras gave up his attempts to get their attention and retreated as quickly as he could.

The footfalls of the Gul'nog horde shook the earth. Twenty meters away they still came at full speed, their feet pounding the hardened dirt like the hooves of stampeding cattle. Weapons wouldn't be necessary, Peter thought. They'd just run them into the ground. The survivors began to melt away from the oncoming charge.

Then the light flared and gathered into a massive ball, pulsing with power. It seemed alive, like billions of shimmering fireflies. Peter shaded his eyes but couldn't look away. The ball of light rose higher, grew brighter and more blinding, until the attackers were only ten

meters away, then it launched itself at the Gul'nog like a flash of brilliant lightning.

The creatures yelped in fear and stumbled. Some fell. Others turned and ran. The largest one pulled up in surprise, but he had no fear. He saw his army faltering, so he raised his horn and blew.

It was the same rumbling bellow Peter had heard before. It shook his bones and reverberated in his chest.

The Gul'nog stopped fleeing and rejoined ranks. But they did not advance. The two forces stood in a stalemate, the Aedyn troupe regaining their courage and the Gul'nog shielding their eyes from the light, but not turning in retreat.

Still, Peras's eyes were somehow shrouded in darkness. He had his back to the Gul'nog, and he looked up with hatred at Peter and Julia, lingering on Louisa with a hatred so intense it seemed to spark the air. But he turned to the creatures and shouted, "Back! Let us pass. In the name of the Shadow, let us through!"

The creatures did not move. They looked confused. Then some of them seemed to notice Peras's bindings for the first time, and this caused them to step back. They looked at Louisa with fear, as if she were some kind of witch with powers that could not only bind their strongest ally but possibly do worse to them.

Though none of the Gul'nog had fled, Louisa stepped forward as if no wall of giant ogres stood in her way. Peter and the others followed.

And the Gul'nog moved aside. They backed away and made room. Like Moses walking through the midst of the Red Sea, Louisa and her little army — along with Peras and his handlers — passed through the Gul'nog host and strode toward the volcano.

"I thought I was free of this place forever," Alyce said. The group stopped walking and stared into the entrance at the base of the volcano.

Here was the place where they'd all been slaves under Captain Ceres, where he and the Gul'nog forced them to search for something—the talisman, it turned out. But they hadn't known that. All they had known back then was torture and hopelessness.

Julia looked directly up the slope of the volcano. The eruption had blown out a side of the mountain, flattening trees on the far side of the island and blanketing it in white ash. But the side where they stood looked unchanged. High above, the cone's edge glowed orange and the air shimmered in the heat where lava continued to flow. Before them, the tunnel opened like a portal to nothingness. The light from the talisman surrounded the group, but barely illuminated the jagged edges of the rock walls ahead. Were they really going in there? Did the Shadow really reside inside?

Would any of them come out alive?

Foolish thought, Julia.

In her mind's eye Julia saw Gaius. He gave no indication of what she should do. He merely stood there, still as a pond.

Strangely enough, the image gave her confidence. He wasn't upset. He wasn't worried. He remained calm, as if things were going exactly as planned. Julia decided she could share in that same peace.

She turned to look over the plain they'd just crossed. The Gul'nog had not followed, but neither had they left. They sat about in a black cluster half a kilometer back, guarding the only way out.

At the rear of her people, her Aedyn family, Peter, Mitchell, Kelman, and several others walked with Peras. They'd bound his arms again and reapplied the gag, but Julia still didn't feel safe with him there.

She heard Alexander whimpering. The boy held his mother's hand over his ear and seemed to be trying to merge into her leg.

Louisa saw too. She knelt before him and whispered into his ear. Something she said evidently surprised him, because he jerked his head up to look at Alyce, and then back at Louisa. He sprang away from his mother and grabbed Louisa's hand. Together, they strode toward the cave that waited before them.

Julia didn't know what Louisa had said or promised, but it must've been good. With Gaius in her mind's eye and the light of the Lord of Hosts around her, she, too, stepped into the abyss. Peter and the others followed.

The tunnel delved straight into the belly of the volcano. Oddly, it wasn't hot in the tunnel, as Julia had thought an active volcano certainly would be. The tunnel they walked through was roughly circular, like a tube, and tall enough for them to walk through standing upright. Julia looked back in time to see the daylight at the mouth of the tunnel disappear from view. Now only this strange light that surrounded them lit their way and kept them safe. It was almost chilly in the tunnel.

The group walked deeper, their path slanted downward, further than any of them had ever dug, until the darkness felt thick but for the ever-present light coming from the talisman. They reached a bend in the tunnel. Julia shuddered to think what she would do if the talisman were lost.

What *was* the light? It wasn't actually coming from the talisman, or there would be no light behind Louisa, because she wore it on her chest. It would shine only where she happened to be facing. But the light seemed more like a balloon of brightness around them.

"Stay together," Julia said to no one and everyone, though she couldn't imagine anyone intentionally straying far.

They walked along in eerie silence. Julia had not expected to hear sounds of animals or nature down here, but the absence of sound started to scare her. It wasn't natural for there to be silence this deep. She felt the darkness on either side of their light bubble and the massive, erupting volcano above them and wished for a giant falcon to whisk her away home.

She was amazed that she wasn't hungry or thirsty or tired, even after so much walking and so little sleep. If Julia needed another sign that the Lord of Hosts was with them, that was it.

Louisa stopped.

Julia looked around. Before her eyes could tell her what the problem was, her skin did. She felt a warm breeze. And not from in front or behind them, but from the side.

They were standing at a crossroads. Five smaller tunnels branched out from here. Some sloped upward, some downward, others stayed level. Just inside one of the tunnels, two more tunnels branched off.

"Now what?" Priscilla asked.

Julia was wondering the same thing. She sent up a prayer to the Lord of Hosts. If they were here on His business doing His will against His enemies, then He could be called upon to help make it happen.

She almost grinned at the thought. Was this what faith felt like?

Louisa, who was standing at Julia's right shoulder, began to hum. It was a tune Julia recognized. In fact, it was *the* tune for which Louisa had become known. With no visible signal, Louisa, Julia, and the entire Aedyn group began to sing:

The two come together; the two become one;
With union comes power, control over all

Flooded by light, the shadow outdone,
The host shall return; the darkness shall fall.

Only Peras didn't join in the singing. He seemed to cringe away from the words. It occurred to Julia that he seemed to cringe away from the light too. And Louisa. And Julia, Peter, Mitchell, Kelman, and just about everyone and everything else. What must be going through his mind? If he went out to the Gul'nog, would they welcome him or tear him to pieces?

As the song continued, Julia tried to puzzle out the meaning of the words.

The two coming together and becoming one — that probably meant the lands of Aedyn and Khemia coming under one group's authority. She'd at first thought that was Captain Ceres trying to expand his domain. But with Ceres gone, perhaps it was the Gul'nog that wanted more land. Or perhaps the Shadow wanted all of it for itself.

The next line, about union and power over all, seemed to belong with that first part. Someone bad wanted to conquer and control. If the slavery these people had gone through on Khemia was a taste of that control, Julia didn't want any part of it.

But as dark as the first two lines were, the last two lines outshone them. *Flooded by light.* Julia looked around. Yes, that's what she was seeing here, and what she'd seen when the Gul'nog horde had attacked. Would the Shadow really be outdone? If it said so in the song, it had to be true. She hoped.

The host returning ... could that mean the Lord of Hosts or the population of Aedyn? Some couldn't return, because they were dead. But maybe this meant Aedyn could become repopulated in time. And the idea of the darkness falling was altogether wonderful, whatever it meant.

The song ended, and its last notes echoed down corridors that had perhaps never heard the sound of the good news of the Lord of Hosts.

As if someone had whispered the precise directions into her ear, Louisa marched with certainty into the second corridor on their right. The others followed without pause. Some hummed the song again. Julia didn't know how Louisa could tell this was the right way, but she didn't question it for a second.

However, if it *was* the correct path, each step brought them closer to the Shadow.

CHAPTER

14

Each time the group came to a narrow hole they could barely squeeze through, each switchback that seemed to lead in circles, each bottomless hole they had to hop across, Peter's doubt grew. Now that they stood before another set of tunnels, Peter desperately wanted to ask, *Louisa, how did you know which tunnel to take?* What if they were lost? He was completely befuddled. They'd passed so many offshoot tunnels, and they'd been down here so long—or had it been long at all? He wouldn't be able to find his way back if he'd wanted to. Every time, Louisa had seemed to know flawlessly which one to take. But what if she was just doing that to keep everyone fooled? What if the light had only so many hours of use before it went out? What if they were suddenly plunged into darkness? They would die down here and no one would ever find their bones.

Louisa leaned close to him, as though she'd read his mind. "I take a step in a direction, and if the light goes with me, I know it's the right way."

Peter stared at her. Was she kidding? That was her process?

She looked at him in that enigmatic way of hers and moved directly into the tunnel on the left. It went steeply downward.

Peter followed with the rest of the group, but he did so mainly because Louisa held the only light in Peter's universe right now. He wasn't going to strike off on his own.

He thought of his life back in England. He didn't really have any friends there who would miss him. Certainly his school wouldn't mourn the loss of a problem student. Father was probably jumping for joy to be rid of the family disgrace. His stepmother would probably throw a party. The only thing that would ruin her mood would be if he actually returned. Despite the light all around him, it was funny how his thoughts could plunge into darkness.

That was when he realized he couldn't see.

The walls had vanished—or else the light had gone out. He knew it! They were abandoned deep beneath the ...

No, wait. How strange! He could still see the others. Louisa stood there, all but glowing in the light of the talisman around her neck. Julia was there too, looking straight up. The others spun all around and gasped.

The reasonable part of Peter's brain tried to work it out. How could he see some things but not others? He looked down—the rock floor was there.

Think, Peter. Your eyes are working. You can see people around you. So you're not blind. And you haven't fallen into a bottomless pit because you can still see the floor—and you're not falling.

So if you can see others and you can see the floor but you can't see the walls or the ceiling...

"We're in a cavern," he said aloud. His voice didn't bounce back to him in that comfortable way he'd gotten used to in the tunnel. It simply disappeared, as if absorbed by the nothingness.

"It must be huge," Trevor said. "The light doesn't reach the edges or the top."

Alyce caught her breath. "The entire population of Aedyn could fit in here."

"Mommy," Alexander said. "If it weren't so far from the outside, maybe we could move here!"

Peter looked at him. The boy was a lot braver than Peter felt.

Mitchell pointed to Peter's left. "Is it my imagination, or does it sort of glow over that way?"

"I can't tell," Kelman said, joining him. "Whenever I look right at it, it's all black. But if I look off somewhere else, I think I see light in the corner of my eye."

Louisa spun all around, her arms spread wide. "We are here."

Peter's heart sank. Where better for Shadow to dwell than in a darkness that even the light of the Lord of Hosts could not penetr—

"Where is he?!" It was Kelman, and he sounded worried.

Mitchell ran through the group, searching this way and that.

Ice ran through Peter's veins. "Louisa! Peras is missing. Everyone, find Peras!"

Instead of searching, they clumped more tightly together. Alexander ran into Alyce's arms. Julia gravitated to Peter's side. Gregory and Orrin and Trevor looked around anxiously. Peter even thought he saw a flicker of something on Louisa's—

From the darkness beyond the reach of the light came a scraping sound.

"What was that?"

Mitchell ran toward it. "It has to be Peras. Come on!"

Peter took a step that way too, but then Limas cried out behind him, "No, wait! Peras is over here."

Peter and Mitchell froze. They were at the very edge of the light. Peter could see only the outline of Mitchell's face and shoulder.

They heard the scraping sound again. Closer.

The first time, it had sounded like a dry stick broom being pulled across a stone floor. This time, it sounded like claws scouring over volcanic rock. Big claws.

An image of the giant falcon that had brought them to Aedyn popped into Peter's thoughts. But the falcon in his imagination now was hateful and ate the flesh of English schoolboys.

Peter grabbed Mitchell and trotted back toward the group. "You found Peras? Where?"

Limas pointed to a lump Peter could barely see at the *other* edge of the light.

"Is he asleep?" Peter asked.

"Maybe he fell," Gregory said, coming to stand beside Peter.

No one moved. In the gloom, the lump could be Peras—it certainly looked like him—but it could be some other nightmarish creature as well.

Someone cried out in the back of the group, "Did you hear that scratching? What's out there?"

Peter turned back to Peras ... just in time to see him expand in size. The creature-that-used-to-be-Peras rose to his full height, or higher. Though he faced away from them, it was clear that his arms and legs were no longer bound. Peras whipped something off his head — the gag — and turned to them. Silver flashed in his hand.

A woman in the group behind them screamed softly, whether from the appearance of Peras or something else on the other side, Peter didn't know. He felt like screaming himself.

Peras stepped toward them, and with every step his form became clearer. Here was the very antithesis of their savior. His heroic golden hair now looked like a web of black coils. His glistening muscles now looked like the sinews of a torturer. And in his newly healed right hand, he held a knife.

Peter's knife.

The group cried out as one. Something about the sound made it clear that it was not the appearance of Peras that caused their screaming. Though Peter feared turning his back on Peras, he had to see what had emerged from the cavern.

All at once, the darkness on the other side of the group seemed to move, as if it had never been a void at all but the light-swallowing back of a massive creature.

The scratching sound gathered and exploded into the sound of solid rock being torn apart like cloth.

The form in the darkness rose and rose and rose like a volcano of darkness. Peter couldn't see it exactly, but he felt it, heard it, smelled it. It was the smell of incinerated bones. The form coiled around the group in a vortex of sludge-like blackness. Peter's last hope of explaining it scientifically fell away.

Peter glanced at Peras and was surprised to see that Peras looked confused too. As shocked as everyone.

Peras lifted his arms and looked at the ground, as if he felt something sneaking around behind him.

"Who ..."

The sound—was it a voice or a black wind? It came from all around, but loudest from the direction where they'd first thought they'd seen Peras.

"Who dares ...?" it said. "Who dares come to the foundation of darkness?"

Peter tried to locate the source of the sound. But every time he thought he saw something and spun toward it, there was only blackness. Then Peter would see something in another direction, but it, too, would be gone when he looked toward it. The creature was insubstantial and murky, truly nothing but Shadow. All Peter was left with were vague images, but they were enough.

Claw. Fang. Eye. Maw. At once everywhere and nowhere.

Peter noticed Louisa striding forward, away from the group. She held the talisman in one hand, lifted toward the darkness as if shining a lantern over a dark lake. It seemed to focus the light where she pointed it.

"We dare!" she said, and though she did not shout, her voice nevertheless resonated in the chamber. The Shadow flinched away from her voice and the beam of light emanating from the talisman. "We come to the foundation of darkness because we serve the Light!"

The Shadow shrieked. The sound of its anger scraped at the edges of their light shield like a tornado trying to find the leverage to uproot a house.

"We come in the name of the Lord of Hosts!" Louisa cried. "We come in the name of Him who will take back this land for the light."

The black whirlwind circled around them, but it seemed to ease. Not that the storm was losing power, but that it had ... relaxed? The voice almost chuckled, and that was a sound more frightening than its shrieking.

"You have no weapons," it said. "You have nothing to fight me. You think because you defeated my lords in Aedyn you can defeat me too?" The chuckle returned. "I have taken this land for myself, and I will rule it for ten thousand years."

Louisa looked about calmly, as if she faced off against supernatural forces of darkness every other day. "No," she said simply. "You will retreat. We *do* have weapons. We have the power of the Lord of Hosts. We have each other. And we have the certainty of our calling."

With that, she swung the talisman around, and the light flared. Louisa turned to Julia and took her hand. She looked from Julia to Peter and began to sing. Everyone clasped hands and sang with her.

The two come together...

Peter and the others joined in, and it felt as if the Lord of Hosts was surrounding each of them with a powerful shield. *No.* Peter thought. *It is like the Lord of Hosts has arrived and has filled the cavern with His power.* With wonderment, Peter continued singing the song.

… the two become one…

The Shadow wasn't relaxed anymore. It writhed and shrieked and increased its speed. The sound of wind and scratching swelled until it sounded like a thousand ice picks scraping at the surface of the light shield. The small group's voices rose louder.

With union comes power, control over all;
Flooded by light, the shadow outdone,
The host shall return; the darkness shall fall.

When Louisa reached the end of the song, she immediately began it over again, and the others stayed with her.

Motion on Peter's right caught his eye.

Peras seemed to shake out of some kind of stupor. He looked around as if waking from sleepwalking. He looked at the people, the light shield, and the Shadow outside. He lowered his head and covered his ears, as if hearing the Shadow's shrieks for the first time. But when he raised his hands to his ears, he saw the knife in his hand. He turned it this way and that like it was the first knife he'd ever seen.

Then his posture seemed to harden, and he gripped the knife firmly. He looked up at the group again, and his eyes found Louisa. He stepped forward, pushing men out of the way as if they were cobwebs.

Peter couldn't move. He couldn't speak. His mind wanted him to throw himself at Peras, or at least cry out, but all he could do was watch in horror as this muscular assassin stalked closer to Louisa.

Alyce saw Peras coming and cried out. Others spun to see, but they would be too late.

Louisa turned toward him, a look of utter peace on her face, the words of the song of the Lord of Hosts on her lips.

Peras drew back his hand to strike.

Julia screamed.

At the sound, whatever had been holding Peter back was suddenly gone, and he found himself running forward. "No!"

But he was too far away. He needed two seconds to cross the distance, but Peras needed only one more step.

"*No!*"

The knife flashed forward.

Peras stumbled. It threw off his aim. He missed. He sidestepped to recover, but tripped again.

Peter didn't slow down to see what had tripped him. He had time now! He launched himself at Peras.

Though Peter was barely half Peras's height and less than half his weight, Peras was so off-balance that

Peter's weight sent him tumbling away from the light and toward the vortex swirling outside of it.

Peras dropped the knife in his fall and landed sprawling right at the edge of the light shield.

He stood up, enraged. He whipped around toward Peter, and Peter saw in Peras's face the same fury he'd seen on the rafts.

Peras roared and spread his arms like a bear. His bulging muscles seemed to double in size. Veins surfaced across his body. He grew nearly a foot taller, and he straightened to his full height.

His eyes, which had never fully returned to their baby-blue innocence, transformed once more into vile, bottomless black irises that seemed to channel the Shadow directly.

"You will see," Peras said, though his was now the voice of the Shadow, "that I have weapons too. One that stands inside your precious light!"

"Oh," Louisa said, as if just noticing the problem. "Well, we can easily deal with that." With a flick of her wrist, which held the talisman, the edge of the light shield moved, changing its shape.

And now Peras was outside of it.

For a moment, Peras appeared confused again. Despite his new size and monstrous appearance, he seemed befuddled. He reached toward the shield, but his hands struck it as if it were solid and not just a bright light. He pushed it. He struck it. He pounded on it. His face clouded and he flew into a rage, stepping back and slamming himself against it with enough force to break through stone walls.

Peter stood and rejoined the group. Someone else was getting up too, and Peter realized that this person must've been what Peras had tripped over.

But the body was very small.

"Alexander?" Peter said.

The boy smiled at him as if he'd just slain a dragon. Maybe he had. Again Peras threw himself into the shield, and again it held.

Louisa sang.

The two come together; the two become one ...

Peter looked at Julia. She had tears on her cheeks, but the look on her face was now one of tentative hope. She joined Louisa in song, as did Peter and the others.

With union comes power, control over all ...

Outside the shield, the Shadow stopped spinning. Two points of glowing orange floated in the dark cavern, swaying side to side as if made of smoke. Or like the hypnotic stare of the cobra.

Peras ceased trying to burst through the shield. He turned his back to the group and looked instead into the eyes and fangs of the Shadow. "No, please." He pressed his back against the shield and slid sideways. "I tried. You saw."

The Shadow's face shimmered with undulations of smoke. It moved high above Peras, and Peter thought he saw a flash of its profile. It looked like a dragon of myth. Or a crocodile. Lengthened face, jutting lower jaw, giant malformed fangs crisscrossing in a soul-shredding smile.

"You failed," the Shadow said. It sounded less like a statement and more like a judgment.

Peras ran. In five steps he could no longer be seen. But the Shadow had no trouble tracking him in the darkness. The dark shape swiveled and struck down-ward with the speed of a snake.

Flooded by light, the shadow outdone,
The host shall return; the darkness shall fall.

As Louisa led them into another round of the song, Peter searched the darkness. The cavern seemed empty again. Could that be it? Would the Shadow be satisfied with punishing the failure of one of its servants? Would it now leave them al—

Something slammed against the roof of the light shield.

The group cried out in alarm and bent their knees, as if bracing for the volcano to fall on their heads.

Something heavy and dark lay on the top of the shield. But it didn't have the right angles to be rock or the right consistency to be lava. It was indistinct at first, but then Peter saw a shape he recognized.

A human hand. Then the arm and body to which it was connected. Large muscles ... black coils that transformed into blond strands.

Peras. His body pressed against the surface of the shield, restored to its human proportions. He tried to stand to his feet.

Then suddenly he flew away. Or, rather, was lifted away. His body vanished like it had never been there.

Wham.

Peras's body slammed against the shield behind the group. It didn't linger there this time, but was lifted away again. The scratching resumed, and the vortex began spinning faster.

Wham, wham, wham.

Peter was appalled. The Shadow was using Peras's body as a blunt instrument to beat against the shield in search of a weak spot.

Peter lost track of the hammering. Peras became a soggy indistinct mass.

As Peras's body oozed down the slope of the shield, Peter closed his eyes, and his logical mind made a feeble attempt to understand this protection surrounding them. A clear dome stood overhead, a shield created by the power of the Lord of Hosts. Peter put his logical mind back to sleep for a while.

He didn't pity Peras. The man—if a man he was—had chosen darkness. He had betrayed them all more than once and had come a hair's breadth away from killing Louisa. He probably would have killed the rest of them as well. But Peter couldn't imagine the fear and pain of being slammed around by a frustrated manifestation of evil.

As it had before, the Shadow plucked up Peras's body. But it seemed a more violent withdrawal this time, and Peter glimpsed Peras being hurled away. Several seconds passed, during which the group neared the end of the song again. Then Peter heard, or imagined he heard, the soft *whump* of a body landing in a heap far away.

So ended the brief but fearsome reign of Peras the Betrayer.

Peter saw the bodiless face of the Shadow again. Its eyes shone like twin coals removed from a raging furnace. Somehow it looked even more furious than before.

Louisa looked directly at Peter. "Now we must sing our strongest!"

The two come together; the two become one ...

The Shadow bellowed. Its face rose high over them.

With union comes power, control over all ...

The twin orange glows shattered, exploding out to empower the black fog. It spun around them anew. The scratching increased. But it was no longer merely wind and sound. Flotsam rotated in the cloud now. Volcanic rock. Stalactites. Boulders. Molten rock that splintered upon impact with the shield.

Flooded by light, the shadow outdone ...

Boulders the size of train engines fell against the shield.

Suddenly, Limas was shouting in Peter's face. "It's bringing the mountain down on us!"

The sound of multiple heavy impacts against the shield drummed like an avalanche. The debris began to pile up all around the edge of the shield. The Lord of Hosts might keep them from being crushed—but would they be buried alive? Would they be stuck down here forever, alive but never free?

Peter saw pinpricks of fire in the chaos outside the shield. At first he thought they were splashes of lava breaking against their dome. But they didn't fall ... they floated and spun and grew.

Julia's face swam in front of him. "It's the Shadow," she said, though she looked like she was shouting. "It's burning up from the inside!"

Peter looked back out into the maelstrom. Could she be right? Her proposed solution fit the evidence, but how could she possibly know? Around him, the people of Aedyn stood or crouched or sat on the ground, observing it all like people watching a building fire. In shock and unable to do anything but watch.

And sing.

The host shall return; the darkness shall fall.

Instead of starting the song over, as she'd done so many times before, Louisa sang the last line again. And again.

The host shall return; the darkness shall fall.
The host shall return; the darkness shall fall.
The host shall return; the darkness shall fall.

The sparks of flame enlarged until they merged into one another. Until there was more flame than darkness. Until there was only flame.

The Shadow shrieked and the tornado became a hurricane of fire. Tongues of flame flashed over the shield like an explosion, like a slush of scalding embers spraying from a furnace, like exhaust from the very core of the sun.

Then, with a scream so loud Peter dropped to the ground into a ball and wept, the Shadow fell silent and everything went dark.

Peter covered his head, though he knew it would do nothing against the landslide that would crush him now that the shield had failed.

But nothing struck him. He waited, still clenched against the weight that would fall. Nothing came. He opened his eyes. Or perhaps his eyes were already open. Either way, he couldn't see anything.

Am I dead?

He heard rustling around him. The sound of movement. Then whispers and groans of fear.

"Arise, men and women of Aedyn." It was Louisa's voice. She sounded strong.

Peter lifted his head and turned toward her voice. "Louisa?"

"You have prevailed, servants of the Lord of Hosts," Louisa said. "The Shadow is no more!"

As if it had been planned, at her words a light flared above them. But it wasn't the talisman or even the shield.

It was sunlight.

CHAPTER
15

Julia blinked at the golden light streaming into the side of the volcano. It had to be late morning or early afternoon. But what day was it?

The light bathed them all in its friendly glow. Around her she saw the survivors of Aedyn. She helped Alyce and Alexander to their feet, then went to Peter. He seemed fine—but was as amazed as she felt, judging from his wide-open eyes.

Julia went to Louisa then. She was the only one who didn't seem to have spent any time on the ground.

Louisa placed the cord of the talisman over her neck and let it rest against her chest again. "Well," she said. "That was an adventure."

Julia laughed. The laughter burst out of her like something between a guffaw and a sob, and it loosened a landslide of tears and chuckles, both in her and several of those around her.

Alexander tugged on Louisa's hand. "Healer, you're hurt."

Louisa looked at the back of her hand. A cut a couple of centimeters long stretched along the base of her right hand. "Oh, so I am. Wonder how that happened."

Alexander took Louisa's hand in both of his and looked at it intently. Then he placed his face over the wound. Julia couldn't see what he was doing—was he kissing it? When he withdrew his head, the cut was gone.

Louisa laughed then. She lifted her face to the sunlight and laughed as if the Lord of Hosts had played a marvelous joke on her to make her happy. She swept Alexander into her arms and hugged him. "I knew it!"

A thought struck Julia, and she looked up. The sun was high overhead, but beaming right at them. "Everyone," she said, pointing. "The dark cloud—it's gone!"

The group looked up and gasped. Julia saw them all staring upward together and thought they looked like sunflowers gazing at the sun, basking in its warmth and love.

She couldn't actually be certain the whole shadowy cloud was gone, but it was the first time since the eruption that she'd been able to see sun and sky directly overhead. She had a feeling the shadow was completely burned away. As if to confirm her guess, her face was brushed by something else she hadn't enjoyed in a long time: a breeze of fresh air.

The group stood in a circle, holding one another, looking around. The debris of the Shadow's passing lay about them in a perfect circle. Heaps of rock surrounded their open spot like the walls of a crater.

She saw Peter bend down and pick something up from the ground. He laughed and walked over to Gregory. "Here," Peter said. "This is yours. I took it for the rafts when you were injured. I'm afraid it's had an adventure all its own."

Julia couldn't see what it was, but Gregory chuckled, looked it over, and stuck it in his belt. Then she saw. Gregory's knife.

Peter looked at her and smiled. He stepped closer and took her hand. Together they walked to Louisa, and the three of them joined hands.

"I don't know what we'll find out there," Peter said, "but do you two have the same feeling I do, that our work here is finished—or nearly so?"

Julia nodded. "I do."

Louisa had a faraway look in her eyes, but she finally nodded. When she did, she seemed to deflate. "You're probably right."

Julia thought she looked almost sad. "Still," she said, trying to guess Louisa's mood. "It will be sad to leave. Here, we were deliverers and healers and heroes of mighty conflicts. There, we're just schoolchildren."

Louisa stared away again. And then, with the deepest sigh Julia had ever seen her give, Louisa picked Alexander up again and headed toward the tumble of rocks leading up to the hole in the side of the volcano. "Come, everyone. Let's begin. It's time to walk again in the light."

Despite the fact that the landslide had only just come to rest on the floor of the cavern, it proved remarkably stable as a staircase. Alexander was able to make the climb with no problem — and even Trevor didn't have to rest any more than the others.

The group ended up finding a rift in the volcano wall much lower down than the hole they'd first seen the sun through, so the climb wasn't very long. All the way up, Julia had scanned the floor of the cavern. She wasn't sure what she was looking for: Peras's body, the remains of the Shadow, maybe even Captain Ceres. But all she ever saw were rocks upon rocks.

Julia was the first to scramble up the final step into the open air. What she saw stunned her so deeply she didn't warn anyone else. One by one the people of Aedyn climbed out and stood staring in stunned silence.

It was as if the volcano had never happened. What had been wasteland was now a living paradise. The greenest forest Julia had ever seen stretched over the island like a lush blanket. A cloud of low fog clung to the treetops as if the Lord of Hosts had just created all of this and it was still steaming a bit from being in an oven. The shadow was indeed gone. There was no sign of it anywhere. Clouds lazed overhead, promising a glorious sunset in a few hours.

Julia looked up the slope of the volcano. It seemed impossible, but it looked as if it hadn't erupted in a thousand years. The slopes looked old and gray. There were no rivers of molten lava. No heat shimmering off the cone. No ash or smoke leaked—much less spewed— out of the top.

Julia cast her eyes to the horizon. Sunlight sparkled off the ocean like diamonds on a vast blue tablecloth. In the direction of Aedyn, she could make out a green shape toward the edge of her vision that seemed to float like a living vessel.

The plain they'd crossed before, upon which they'd faced the Gul'nog battle line, was overgrown with beautiful trees that swayed gently in the ocean wind. The Gul'nog themselves were gone. Her mind went to all the people of Aedyn who had fallen on this island—

in the slave mines and at the cave during the Gul'nog attack. She had to believe that the Lord of Hosts had cared for their bodies when He renewed this place.

Julia found Louisa and Peter on either side of her. They didn't speak. They just stared together at what the Lord of Hosts had done.

At length, someone pressed something into Julia's hand. Gregory smiled at her. It was a luscious-looking pear.

"Fruit trees," he said, sweeping his hand over their view of the island. "The place is filled with them." He took a monstrous bite out of another pear. "And it's a good thing too, because all of a sudden my hunger has returned!"

They spent the next twenty minutes feasting on fruit of many kinds and enjoying the open air. Kelman and Orrin stretched out on the grassy slope and napped. Priscilla and Alyce and Imogene wove flowers into their hair. Peter and his raftsmen talked about the new rafts they were going to build—with paddles and rudders and even sails this time—to get the people back to Aedyn.

Julia found herself looking around for Gaius. This was about the time he usually showed up. But he was nowhere to be found. The Lord of Hosts had been so visible when they'd first come to Aedyn. His power and presence and voice were with them all the time then, it seemed. But the longer they'd stayed, the more He hid. The signs of His presence were still there, and sometimes quite powerfully, but they had turned more covert, more subtle.

Maybe that's what it means to live in faith, she thought. *Maybe you need the big signs of His love at first, but then He shows you how to see Him in the quiet ways. But no matter how He appears, He's still guiding, still there.*

"What's that, Mother?" Alexander asked, pointing into the sky.

Julia followed his gaze. She saw a black speck against the blue dome of the sky. It wasn't possible to see any distinct shape yet, but she knew in her heart what it was.

Peter said it for her. "It's the falcon."

Louisa nodded. "Come to take us home."

Julia looked at them all. Her brother, her step-sister, Gregory, and the people who had come to be more than family to her. This was it, then. This was the end.

As the speck grew nearer, and it became clear that it was indeed the giant falcon, Julia and the others said their good-byes. Each of them seemed to have one person they saved for last.

Peter came last to Trevor, though Mitchell, Orrin, and Kelman stood close by.

"I have heard it said that soldiers who endure battle together become brothers," Peter said, clasping Trevor's forearms. "You men are like brothers to me now. I fear I will never see you again. Though it is not rational in the least to say this—you will always, *always* live in my heart."

Louisa came last to Alexander. She knelt before the boy and held him in her lap, while Alyce stood nearby.

"Alexander," Louisa said. "You must take my place now."

He looked confused. "What do you mean, healer?"

"*That's* what I mean," Louisa said with a wise smile. She slipped the cord of the talisman off her neck and put it around Alexander's. "You are the healer now, dear boy. I knew the Lord of Hosts was preparing you for this when we worked together to heal the wounded before." She looked up at Alyce. "But I think He was preparing me too, because if there were no healer to take my place, I fear I would not be willing to leave." She met Julia's eyes. "Though there is healing yet for me to do at home."

Julia didn't know entirely what that meant, but she had no time to contemplate it, as she was now standing before her last farewell: Gregory.

She knew she was too young for romance, and Gregory was too old for her in any case. But here was the man who would forever hold the place in her heart as her first love. As Peter had said about soldiers going through battle together, so she felt connected to Gregory.

A thought struck her: if time passed differently in her world than in this one, could she somehow use that to "catch up" to Gregory? The math of it began to hurt her head, and for once she wished for Peter to tell her the science, but she thought that if she went through the portal and came back at the right time ... Or did she need to send him through and she stay here?

But as he looked at her with kindness in his eyes, she knew it wasn't to be. She would just have to find a Gregory in her world.

"Julia," he said, "I had an … interesting time with you on our adventure. You are twice the warrior I'll ever be, and you do it with such grace it's hard to believe you're so young. I will indeed miss you, my friend."

She wanted to say something fitting in reply, but she felt tears welling in her eyes, so she settled for giving him an enormous hug. He returned it warmly, and they stood like this for a full minute.

And then, in a *whoosh* of mighty wings that sent pebbles scattering, the falcon landed in their midst. Some reached out and petted its side.

The noble creature folded its wings away and looked at Julia with a canny gaze. "It is time to return, children of Earth."

Even though she knew it had been coming, Julia didn't want to go. Who would want to return to a life of being a nobody when she could stay and be known as a hero?

The falcon seemed to guess her thoughts. "There are adventures yet to face," it said. "You three have done well here. The children of Aedyn will rebuild. The Lord of Hosts has them in His hand. But you three are needed elsewhere."

Louisa was first to climb upon the falcon's back. Peter followed. He climbed into the nook behind its neck and gave his men a victory wave. Then, with a longing look at all her friends, Julia joined them atop the great

bird. She opened her mouth to give some great parting thought, but the falcon sprang into the air.

A distance away from the volcano, as the falcon's mighty wings propelled them higher, Julia caught sight of something brown in a field of green. She thought at first it was a fallen log, but when she looked closer she saw it was not.

It was Gaius. Standing in his monk's robe. His arm raised in farewell.

Julia shook her head at the Lord of Hosts's sense of humor. *Good-bye, Gaius,* she thought. *Thank you for everything.*

With that, the falcon swerved toward the sea. They were headed home.

CHAPTER

16

"We'd better go in, don't you think?"

Peter, Julia, and Louisa stood looking at their house. It was nighttime, just as it had been when they'd left. They actually had no idea how much time had passed here. It could be mere hours since they'd left, or it could be days or decades.

Still, the house looked the same. Snow packed its roof and eaves, and the yard remained covered in a blanket of white. Smoke rose from the chimney, and yellow light shone through the windows. But it was hard to see details of the house in the dark and from this distance. It could be fifty years later and about to fall apart. The line of trees they were standing in, right at the edge of their lawn, looked no larger or older than when they'd left. That had to mean something.

Peter looked behind them into the woods from which they'd come. The falcon had set them down at the frozen creek where they'd entered Khemia. It looked exactly the same as before. Peter even thought he'd spotted some of his own footprints in the snow.

He turned to Julia. "You're sure? When you came back to get the pendant, Stepmother didn't ask you where Louisa was? She only asked where I was?" He looked back at the house. "That doesn't seem right."

Julia nodded. "I'm quite sure, Peter. She scolded me for being 'a little heroine' and running away. She asked me to tell her where you were, Peter, because Father was still out looking for you." She grimaced. "I'm sorry, Louisa, but she didn't mention you at all. I can only think it meant she hadn't realized you were missing yet."

Louisa looked especially cold. She hunched her shoulders and clasped the collar of her garment right under her chin. "It's all r-right. M-maybe we haven't been gone v-very long."

"Well, I don't know about you two," Peter said, "but I've gotten used to island temperatures. Someone's got a fire going in that house, and I say we go get close to it."

"I ag-gree."

They'd taken two steps across the frozen lawn when a commotion arose around the front of the house. The sound of several people tramping up the steps, knocking on the door, and voices raised came to their ears.

Curious, Peter changed course and went around the side of the house to see what was happening. Julia and Louisa followed, sticking to the shadows.

On the stoop stood a trio of constables talking with Father, Stepmother, and Bertram, Louisa's brother.

"Nothing at all in the hospitals?" Father asked.

The lead constable shook his head. "Not a peep, Professor Grant." He pulled out a little notebook and read from it. "No word on your son, Peter, gone these two days, nor on your daughter, Julia, gone, then returned, then gone again." He flipped the notebook closed.

Peter looked at Louisa. Maybe they really didn't know she was gone. Perhaps they'd entered some parallel dimension in which Stepmother didn't have a daughter named—

"But what of my Louisa?" Stepmother cried. She pushed past Father and grabbed the constable's coat by the buttons. "Where is my baby?"

"Mind the uniform, madam, if you please." The constable removed her hands from his coat. "We are continuing our search for all the children, including your daughter, Louisa. Though I should point out to you that if you'd informed us immediately that *three* children had gone missing, our search might have already met with success. As it is, we must change our search parameters from two to three, which has caused us to have to revisit the hospitals, morgues, and prisons."

Stepmother fell into Father's arms. "Morgues? Oh, Oliver, could it be?"

"Of course not, Helen." Father turned to the constables. "You men must be cold. Why don't you come in?"

The three constables looked at one another like they thought it was a very good idea, but they seemed uncertain. "Well, Captain, we really should return to the search."

"Of course," Father said. "But if there's one thing I learned as captain in the Royal Navy, it's that a hot drink makes cold work bearable. Do step inside. Only for a moment."

"Don't mind if we do, Captain."

Peter looked at Julia and Louisa. "Well?"

"G-go!" Louisa said.

Julia nodded. "May as well."

Peter ran through the snow to the front porch. "Wait! We're here!"

There followed such an uproar of screaming and confusion that Peter could not take it all in. Stepmother wailed and cried and scolded. Bertram sulked away to his room. The constables stumbled over one another to record the information, get the word out to call off the search, and get their warm drinks. Father alternated between hugging Peter and Julia and looking cross with them.

But after the initial furor, the constables finally left, Bertram returned, and Stepmother daubed her tears. Father sat Peter, Julia, and Louisa down on the stone hearth in front of the fire, a plaid woolen blanket spread across their knees, and proceeded to pace.

"First, allow me to say that your mother and I — and Bertram — are most gratified to find you safe and sound. You gave us the scare of our lives."

Stepmother huffed. "It's that Peter's fault, Oliver. Carrying my baby away."

"I told you, Mother!" Bertram said, screwing up his face at Peter. "Worthless boy."

Stepmother pointed a finger at Peter vindictively. "You think you have known pain before now? You will find new meaning for the word when your father is done with you. And you as well, little vixen," she said to Julia.

Father nodded. "Quite. Second, this habit of running off at all hours will stop this instant. Your mother and I — "

He continued, but Peter's mind turned inward. *She's not my mother*, he wanted to say. But that was the old Peter talking. He was different now. Things had to change. He watched his father pacing and talking. He was working himself into a froth. He would beat Peter. If he were mad enough, he would beat Julia too.

Lord of Hosts, what am I to do?

"—cost who knows how much to the city to have the whole constabulary out searching for you!" Father said, nearly shouting now. "We'll see it in taxes next, mark my words! And we cannot afford any increase, I tell you!"

Father unbuckled his belt and slid it through the loops on his trousers. It dangled in his hand, a black snake crueler than any Gul'nog blade. Not because it would hurt the flesh more, but because of who wielded it. It would hurt the soul more.

Peter thought back to Peras, a man who had lost his way under the influence of the Shadow. Though it hurt to realize, his father had become just as hate-filled and misled. And this time Peter could not hope for a supernatural light to destroy the shadows that overtook his father's face.

Father's eyes flashed. "Seventh, I will be boxed before I let a son of mine bring dishonor to our family name." He snapped the belt in his hands. "Not while I am master of this house." His voice dropped dangerously. "Stand, Peter."

Julia leapt up, knocking the blanket aside. "No, Father! You mustn't do that! Peter did nothing to dishonor—"

"Silence!" Stepmother said, pushing Julia toward the hearth.

Bertram stuck his foot out, and Julia tripped, tumbling headfirst toward the fire.

Louisa caught her, but Julia's head struck the mesh metal grate in front of the fire and knocked it over. Sparks and heat surged into the room.

Stepmother's mouth dropped open. "Careful, you fool. You'll burn holes in my rug!"

Father pushed Peter aside and yanked Julia from the hearth. "Sit *down!*" he said, forcing her to the carpet.

The look of fear on Julia's face as she looked at her father was enough for Peter.

"All right, that's it." Peter took Julia by the hand and pulled her toward the front door. He placed himself between her and the others. "No one is to strike Julia. Is that understood?"

The shock on Stepmother's face was worth any beating Peter would have to endure. But she quickly recovered. Her angular face turned sharp as a hatchet. "Why, you ungrateful whelp. Oliver, don't just stand there like a git. Show him the back of your belt."

Father readied the belt to strike. "Peter, come away and bend down. Take your licks like a good sailor, and this will be behind us all."

Julia pulled at Peter's shoulder. "Let's go, Peter. We'll come back when he's calmed down."

"No." He shook her hand off his arm. "If you run from a bully, it only makes him bolder."

"A bully?" Stepmother said. "Did you hear that? Give *me* the belt. I'll—"

"I'll do it!"

The way Father stood there, heaving with anger and backlit by the fire, returned Peter's mind to the raft when he'd stood against Peras. No knife this time, but a belt. No open ocean, but a sea of anger flowing toward him.

Peter got out of his fighting stance and stood tall. "I will endure your whipping, Father, because I am your son and because I live in obedience to you as I do to the Lord of Hosts."

Bertram laughed. "Him—obedient?"

Peter looked at Louisa. She was back to the old stepsister, it appeared, and would not help him. Peter looked back at his father. "But if you so much as lay a finger on Julia in anger, she and I will leave your home, and you will never see either of us again."

"Oh!" Stepmother said. "You let him talk to you like that? Your own son?"

Father looked angry, but Peter saw uncertainty in his eyes too, so he pressed his point.

"You have changed, Father. You have been bewitched by this woman's bitterness. You are no longer the father who raised us and worshiped Mother. You have become a monster, a creature of darkness. And believe me, I know what I'm talking about. You can beat me until my back is flayed, but you are done berating us in your anger and fear. Julia and I are your children. Your treasures. But you have forgotten this. And now it will cost you."

Peter lifted his shirt to his shoulders, exposing his back, and leaned against the wall.

Bertram rubbed his hands together greedily, and Stepmother bit her lip in anticipation. Father looked from Peter to Stepmother, then back to Peter. The belt flexed between his hands.

"Go on, then! What are you waiting for?" Stepmother rolled her eyes. "Oh, for the sake of cabbage. Bertie, call the bobbies back. Have to call the constable if you want a real man in this house."

Father spun his face to her. "Enough! I'll do it."

"No, Father," Julia said, pleading.

Father reared back his arm and gave Peter a massive strike of the belt.

Peter cried out, but did not take his arms down or turn away.

"Look, Mother!" Bertram said, clapping. "He drew blood with only one strike! Hit him again, Father!"

Father reared back again, but just as the belt fell, Julia lunged forward. "No!"

The edge of the belt caught Julia across the cheek and arm. She yelped and fell to the ground.

"Julia!" Father said.

Peter stood and rushed at his father. "Never ... strike ... Julia!" He landed on him and they grappled. Peter grabbed the wrist with the belt and wrested it away. They fell over the easy chair and went down in a tangle.

Stepmother screamed. Julia wailed. Bertrand yipped like a terrier and bolted for the kitchen.

Louisa leapt into action at last. She seized a poker from the fireplace and stood on the hearth with a terrible scream. *"Stop it, all of you!"*

So shocked were they by the sound of her voice that they did actually all stop. They began to circle around her as she brandished the poker like a sword. Peter stood over his father, the belt in his hand. With an animal growl, he threw the thing away like it was poison. Julia held her cheek with both hands and muffled her cries.

"Mother!" Louisa said. "You should be ashamed of yourself."

"Me? Why, I—"

"Do not talk, Mother. Let me speak." Louisa brought the poker down and held it more like a walking stick. "I don't remember if you have always been a cancer or if it happened lately."

"A cancer? How dare—"

"But I do know you gave the disease to me. I was horrid to Peter and Julia." Louisa looked at them kindly. "Simply *beastly*. Just as you are now, and just as you've made Bertram. But I couldn't see it. I had to be taken away. I had to go on a marvelous adventure to another—" She looked quickly at Peter and Julia. "I had to ... get away to see it. But now it is as clear as a river of lava in a dark cavern. You are ill." Then Louisa looked almost happy. "But I can do something about people in need of healing, you see."

Louisa hopped off the hearth and went to Julia. She put the poker down and gently pulled Julia's hands away from her face, revealing a wide welt that bled along its edges.

At the sight of it, Father moaned and fell to his knees. Peter almost wanted to strike him.

"A father must discipline his children," Louisa said to Father. "It is how they learn. But when anger is the hand that holds the belt, and when your desire to understand your children is replaced by a single-minded rush to punish, you have ceased to be a father, and you have become a monster."

Stepmother gasped. "Why, you little gasbag! You would speak to your f—"

"And a mother who fills her children with bile and turns her husband into a monster ... is no longer a mother, but a vile creature as well." Louisa turned to Julia. "If we are ever to become a family, the monsters and creatures must be driven from the land. And the healing must begin."

Louisa reached forward and touched Julia's face. When she pulled her hand away, the wound was gone.

A silence grasped the room. Stepmother didn't appear able to breathe. Father looked confused, as if his eyes were telling him something his mind couldn't believe. Even Bertram looked less malicious as wonder overtook his face.

"I'm not ...," Father said. "What just ...?"

Louisa walked toward them all, and they backed away from her as if she might burst into flames and ascend into heaven atop a fiery chariot. She turned Peter around and traced her hand along the white-hot stripe across his back. Where she touched, the injury vanished.

This time the reaction was immediate. Father, Stepmother, and Bertram rushed to Peter to inspect his back.

"It's gone!" Father turned to Louisa with something like fear in his eyes. "What did you ...? How did you do that?"

Louisa took Julia's hand and reached for Peter. The three of them stood hand-in-hand, facing the others.

"Something has happened to us," Louisa said. "We have been ... away. It is an adventure you may not believe, but we will tell it to you if you wish. We journeyed to another world, though your ears reject my words, I know. Nevertheless, it is true. Peter and Julia are heroes

there. Deliverers. Chosen of the Lord of Hosts. And I
…" She sighed. "For a time, I was chosen too, as a healer.
Here in this room, I have brought healing to Julia and
Peter, but my heart tells me I will no longer have this
power. I think the Lord of Hosts let me have it once
more to bring you to your senses."

Stepmother turned to Father. "She's off her nut,
Oliver."

"No," Peter said with a nod. "It's true. It was …
incredible."

Julia nodded as well. "Unbelievable, in fact."

"There is a song we learned there," Louisa said. "I
knew the tune here, but I didn't grasp the words until
we went away. It had power in that world. They were
the words of a prophecy. But I think they have meaning
here, as well."

She cleared her throat, and Peter thought she
was going to sing it. But she spoke instead.

"The song told of two that had to become one,
united, for there to be power. When we left here—only
days ago to you, but months for us—our two families
were kilometers apart, though we lived under the same
roof. I was with Mother and Bertram and Stepfather
against Peter and Julia. They were the enemy. But
the Lord of Hosts showed me that He can bring two
together, not in conflict but as a new union that is stronger than either part alone."

She smiled at her mother. "I think I have one final act of healing to do before I can go back to being just a schoolgirl again. I think I have to heal our families and make them one."

Peter looked at Louisa in wonder. Had this been the little tattletale who had once told Julia that no one had ever loved her? When he'd stood there waiting for Father's beating, he'd never once thought Stepmother could be changed. He thought he would receive the whipping and then decide whether to leave home. But if the Lord of Hosts could so completely change Louisa, was anyone—even Stepmother—beyond His reach?

"Mother," Louisa said, "the Lord of Hosts wants to exchange your heart of stone for one of flesh. Bertram, I see the fine man you can become if you will learn the ways of the Lord. And Stepfather—no, *Father*, I see in Peter and Julia the courage and nobility that you put there, that still lies within you."

At those words, unexpectedly, Father burst into tears. "I'm so, so sorry!" He buried his face in his hands and sobbed like he hadn't since Mother's funeral.

And just like that, the mood in the home shifted.

Louisa went and sat in her mother's lap. Bertram joined them, looking unsure and like a normal boy. He sat next to Louisa, and Louisa whispered something into his ear. The look on his face when he pulled away was priceless. He was going to turn out all right. Louisa would see to that.

Julia took Peter's hand and pulled him toward Father. Peter resisted at first. Then hope at seeing his old, loving father return overwhelmed him, and he knelt beside him.

Julia crawled into Father's lap and wiped his tears. Father looked at her timidly, then cupped her face in his hands. He looked at Peter and grasped his shoulder, and in his gaze was something new and kind. Something like admiration.

"Daddy," Julia said.

Father's voice caught as he tried to answer, so he just hummed, "Mmm?"

"When we were … away … I found this piece of jewelry, or machinery, about so-big." She held out her hands. "We called it the talisman. In it was a little hole in the shape of a six-sided star. The talisman wouldn't work if the star pendant wasn't in it. Then I found the pendant, and Peter and I brought it together with the talisman. We slid that star right into the talisman, and wonderful things happened."

A thrill rushed over Peter. He hadn't seen where Julia was headed with this until now. "It's like you and us," he said. "Father, the talisman was broken without the pendant. And the little star pendant was only nice to look at by itself. But when you put the pendant together in its place in the talisman, there was magic."

Father wept again, but in a happy way.

"I think that now," Julia said, "with Louisa's healing and our return, the Lord of Hosts wants to make something wonderful happen with us too. With all of us."

The six of them rocked quietly together, until Stepmother began to hum a little tune. Peter, Julia, and Louisa looked at each other sharply.

"Mother," Louisa said. "What is that tune?"

"I don't really know, darling," she said. "It came to me just now. I think I used to know it long ago."

Louisa smiled at Peter and Julia. "Would you like to learn the words?"

"Yes, I think I would. Do you know them?"

The three heroes of Aedyn smiled. And sang.

The two come together; the two become one;
With union comes power, control over all,
Flooded by light, the shadow outdone,
The host shall return; the darkness shall fall.

The Aedyn Chronicles

Chosen Ones

Alister McGrath

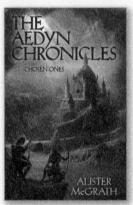

The land of Aedyn is a paradise beyond all imagining. But when this paradise falls, strangers from another world must be called to fight for the truth.

Peter and Julia never suspected that a trip to their grandparents' home in Oxford would contain anything out of the ordinary. But that was before Julia stumbled upon a mysterious garden that shone on moonless nights. It was no accident that she fell into the pool, pulling her brother along with her, but now they're lost in a strange new world and they don't know whom they can trust. Should they believe the mysterious, hooded lords? The ancient monk who appears only when least expected? Or the silent slaves who have a dark secret of their own?

In a world inhabited by strange beasts and magical whisperings, two children called from another world will have to discover who they truly are, fighting desperate battles within themselves before they can lead the great revolution.

The Aedyn Chronicles
Flight of the Outcasts

Alister McGrath

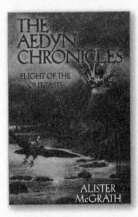

It has been almost a year since Peter and Julia first visited the land of Aedyn and, faced with the harsh reality of their father's remarriage and two new horrible stepsiblings, they're beginning to wonder if it was all a dream. As they run away from home one evening, they fall into a half-frozen river and find themselves back in Aedyn—but this time they've accidentally brought along their stepsister Louisa!

Aedyn is deserted; the people taken captive and forced to work as slaves at the foot of a volcano on a distant island. As Peter and Julia wonder what has happened to their beloved country, a giant falcon appears and takes them to this island, the very place from which the Lord of Hosts saved his people centuries ago. The three children must find a way to save the prisoners and bring them back to Aedyn, but the earth is trembling and the volcano is starting to smoke. They're running out of time.

Available in stores and online!

Share Your Thoughts

With the Author: Your comments will be forwarded to the author when you send them to *zauthor@zondervan.com*.

With Zondervan: Submit your review of this book by writing to *zreview@zondervan.com*.

Free Online Resources at
www.zondervan.com

Zondervan AuthorTracker: Be notified whenever your favorite authors publish new books, go on tour, or post an update about what's happening in their lives at www.zondervan.com/authortracker.

Daily Bible Verses and Devotions: Enrich your life with daily Bible verses or devotions that help you start every morning focused on God. Visit www.zondervan.com/newsletters.

Free Email Publications: Sign up for newsletters on Christian living, academic resources, church ministry, fiction, children's resources, and more. Visit www.zondervan.com/newsletters.

Zondervan Bible Search: Find and compare Bible passages in a variety of translations at www.zondervanbiblesearch.com.

Other Benefits: Register yourself to receive online benefits like coupons and special offers, or to participate in research.

ZONDERVAN

ZONDERVAN.com/
AUTHORTRACKER
follow your favorite authors